Also by John Cheever

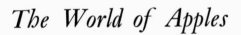

The World of Apples

The World of Apples

JOHN CHEEVER

Alfred A. Knopf New York 1973

THIS IS A BORZOI BOOK
PUBLISHED BY ALFRED A. KNOPF, INC.

Copyright © 1961, 1963, 1964, 1966, 1968, 1970, 1972, 1973
by John Cheever

Library of Congress Cataloging in Publication Data

Cheever, John.
  The world of apples.

  I. Title.
PZ3.C3983WO [PS3505.H6428]   813'.5'2   72–11018
ISBN 0-394-48346-4

The author is grateful for permission to reprint "Montraldo,"
"The Chimera," "Mene, Mene, Tekel, Upharsin," and "Percy,"
which first appeared in *The New Yorker*, "The Fourth Alarm"
and "The World of Apples," which first appeared in *Esquire*,
"The Geometry of Love," which first appeared in *The
Saturday Evening Post*, and "The Jewels of the Cabots,"
"Artemis, the Honest Well Digger," and "Three Stories," which
first appeared in *Playboy*.

Manufactured in the United States of America

FIRST EDITION

Contents

The Fourth Alarm

I sit in the sun drinking gin. It is ten in the morning. Sunday. Mrs. Uxbridge is off somewhere with the children. Mrs. Uxbridge is the housekeeper. She does the cooking and takes care of Peter and Louise.

It is autumn. The leaves have turned. The morning is windless, but the leaves fall by the hundreds. In order to see anything—a leaf or a blade of grass—you have, I think, to know the keenness of love. Mrs. Uxbridge is sixty-three, my wife is away, and Mrs. Smithsonian (who lives on the other side of town) is seldom in the mood these days, so I seem to miss some part of the morning as if the hour had a threshold or a series of thresholds that I cannot cross. Passing a football might do it but Peter is too young and my only football-playing neighbor goes to church.

My wife Bertha is expected on Monday. She comes out from the city on Monday and returns on Tuesday. Bertha is a good-looking young woman with a splendid figure. Her eyes, I think, are a little close together and she is sometimes peevish. When the children were young she had a peevish way of disciplining them. "If you don't eat the nice breakfast mummy has cooked for you before I count three," she would say, "I will send you back to bed. One. Two. *Three. . . .*" I heard it again at dinner. "If you don't eat the nice dinner mummy has cooked for you before I count three I will send you to bed without any supper. One. Two. Three. . . ." I heard it again. "If you don't pick up your toys before mummy counts three mummy will throw them all away. One. Two. Three. . . ." So it went on through the bath and bedtime and one two three was their lullaby. I sometimes thought she must have learned to count when she was an infant and that when the end came she would call a countdown for the Angel of Death. If you'll excuse me I'll get another glass of gin.

When the children were old enough to go to school, Bertha got a job teaching Social Studies in the sixth grade. This kept her occupied and happy and she said she had always wanted to be a teacher. She had a reputation for strictness. She wore dark clothes, dressed her hair simply, and expected contrition and obedience from her pupils. To vary her life she joined an amateur theatrical group. She played the maid in *Angel Street* and the old crone in *Desmonds Acres*. The friends she made in the theater were all pleasant people and I enjoyed taking her to their parties. It is important to know that Bertha does not drink. She will take a Dubonnet politely but she does not enjoy drinking.

Through her theatrical friends, she learned that a nude show called *Ozamanides II* was being cast. She told me this and everything that followed. Her teaching contract gave her ten days' sick leave, and claiming to be sick one day she went into New

4

York. *Ozamanides* was being cast at a producer's office in midtown, where she found a line of a hundred or more men and women waiting to be interviewed. She took an unpaid bill out of her pocketbook, and waving this as if it were a letter she bucked the line saying: "Excuse me please, excuse me, I have an appointment. . . ." No one protested and she got quickly to the head of the line where a secretary took her name, Social Security number, etc. She was told to go into a cubicle and undress. She was then shown into an office where there were four men. The interview, considering the circumstances, was very circumspect. She was told that she would be nude throughout the performance. She would be expected to simulate or perform copulation twice during the performance and participate in a love pile that involved the audience.

I remember the night when she told me all of this. It was in our living room. The children had been put to bed. She was very happy. There was no question about that. "There I was naked," she said, "but I wasn't in the least embarrassed. The only thing that worried me was that my feet might get dirty. It was an old-fashioned kind of place with framed theater programs on the wall and a big photograph of Ethel Barrymore. There I sat naked in front of these strangers and I felt for the first time in my life that I'd found myself. I found myself in nakedness. I felt like a new woman, a better woman. To be naked and unashamed in front of strangers was one of the most exciting experiences I've ever had. . . ."

I didn't know what to do. I still don't know, on this Sunday morning, what I should have done. I guess I should have hit her. I said she couldn't do it. She said I couldn't stop her. I mentioned the children and she said this experience would make her a better mother. "When I took off my clothes," she said, "I felt as if I had rid myself of everything mean and small." Then

I said she'd never get the job because of her appendicitis scar. A few minutes later the phone rang. It was the producer offering her a part. "Oh, I'm so happy," she said. "Oh, how wonderful and rich and strange life can be when you stop playing out the roles that your parents and their friends wrote out for you. I feel like an explorer."

The fitness of what I did then or rather left undone still confuses me. She broke her teaching contract, joined Equity, and began rehearsals. As soon as *Ozamanides* opened she hired Mrs. Uxbridge and took a hotel apartment near the theater. I asked for a divorce. She said she saw no reason for a divorce. Adultery and cruelty have well-marked courses of action but what can a man do when his wife wants to appear naked on the stage? When I was younger I had known some burlesque girls and some of them were married and had children. However, they did what Bertha was going to do only on the midnight Saturday show, and as I remember their husbands were third-string comedians and the kids always looked hungry.

A day or so later I went to a divorce lawyer. He said a consent decree was my only hope. There are no precedents for simulated carnality in public as grounds for divorce in New York State and no lawyer will take a divorce case without a precedent. Most of my friends were tactful about Bertha's new life. I suppose most of them went to see her, but I put it off for a month or more. Tickets were expensive and hard to get. It was snowing the night I went to the theater, or what had been a theater. The proscenium arch had been demolished, the set was a collection of used tires, and the only familiar features were the seats and the aisles. Theater audiences have always confused me. I suppose this is because you find an incomprehensible variety of types thrust into what was an essentially domestic and terribly ornate interior. There were all kinds there that night. Rock music was playing when I came in. It was that deafening old-fashioned kind of Rock they used to play in places like Arthur. At eight thirty the houselights dimmed, and the cast—there were fourteen—came down the aisles. Sure enough, they were all naked excepting Ozamanides, who wore a crown.

I can't describe the performance. Ozamanides had two sons, and I think he murdered them, but I'm not sure. The sex was general. Men and women embraced one another and Ozamanides embraced several men. At one point a stranger, sitting in the seat on my right, put his hand on my knee. I didn't want to reproach him for a human condition, nor did I want to encourage him. I removed his hand and experienced a deep nostalgia for the innocent movie theaters of my youth. In the little town where I was raised there was one—The Alhambra. My favorite movie was called *The Fourth Alarm*. I saw it first one Tuesday after school and stayed on for the evening show. My parents worried when I didn't come home for supper and I was scolded. On Wednesday I played hooky and was able to see the show twice and get home in time for supper. I went to school on Thursday but I went to the theater as soon as school closed and sat partway through the evening show. My parents must have called the police, because a patrolman came into the theater and made me go home. I was forbidden to go to the theater on Friday, but I spent all Saturday there, and on Saturday the picture ended its run. The picture was about the substitution of automobiles for horse-drawn fire engines. Four fire companies were involved. Three of the teams had been replaced by engines and the miserable horses had been sold to brutes. One team remained, but its days were numbered. The

7

men and the horses were sad. Then suddenly there was a great fire. One saw the first engine, the second, and the third race off to the conflagration. Back at the horse-drawn company, things were very gloomy. Then the fourth alarm rang—it was their summons—and they sprang into action, harnessed the team, and galloped across the city. They put out the fire, saved the city, and were given an amnesty by the mayor. Now on the stage Ozamanides was writing something obscene on my wife's buttocks.

Had nakedness—its thrill—annihilated her sense of nostalgia? Nostalgia—in spite of her close-set eyes—was one of her principal charms. It was her gift gracefully to carry the memory of some experience into another tense. Did she, mounted in public by a naked stranger, remember any of the places where we had made love—the rented houses close to the sea, where one heard in the sounds of a summer rain the prehistoric promises of love, peacefulness, and beauty? Should I stand up in the theater and shout for her to return, return, return in the name of love, humor, and serenity? It was nice driving home after parties in the snow, I thought. The snow flew into the headlights and made it seem as if we were going a hundred miles an hour. It was nice driving home in the snow after parties. Then the cast lined up and urged us—commanded us in fact—to undress and join them.

This seemed to be my duty. How else could I approach understanding Bertha? I've always been very quick to get out of my clothes. I did. However, there was a problem. What should I do with my wallet, wristwatch, and car keys? I couldn't safely leave them in my clothes. So, naked, I started down the aisle with my valuables in my right hand. As I came up to the action a naked young man stopped me and shouted—sang—"Put down your lendings. Lendings are impure."

"But it's my wallet and my watch and the car keys," I said.

"Put down your lendings," he sang.

"But I have to drive home from the station," I said, "and I have sixty or seventy dollars in cash."

"Put down your lendings."

"I can't, I really can't. I have to eat and drink and get home."

"Put down your lendings."

Then one by one they all, including Bertha, picked up the incantation. The whole cast began to chant: "Put down your lendings, put down your lendings."

The sense of being unwanted has always been for me acutely painful. I suppose some clinician would have an explanation. The sensation is reverberative and seems to attach itself as the last link in a chain made up of all similar experience. The voices of the cast were loud and scornful, and there I was, buck naked, somewhere in the middle of the city and unwanted, remembering missed football tackles, lost fights, the contempt of strangers, the sound of laughter from behind shut doors. I held my valuables in my right hand, my literal identification. None of it was irreplaceable, but to cast it off would seem to threaten my essence, the shadow of myself that I could see on the floor, my name.

I went back to my seat and got dressed. This was difficult in such a cramped space. The cast was still shouting. Walking up the sloping aisle of the ruined theater was powerfully reminiscent. I had made the same gentle ascent after *King Lear* and *The Cherry Orchard*. I went outside.

It was still snowing. It looked like a blizzard. A cab was stuck in front of the theater and I remembered then that I had snow tires. This gave me a sense of security and accomplishment that would have disgusted Ozamanides and his naked court; but I seemed not to have exposed my inhibitions but to have hit on some marvelously practical and obdurate part of myself. The wind flung the snow into my face and so, singing and jingling the car keys, I walked to the train.

The Jewels
of the Cabots

Funeral services for the murdered man were held in the Unitarian church in the little village of St. Botolphs. The architecture of the church was Bullfinch with columns and one of those ethereal spires that must have dominated the landscape a century ago. The service was a random collection of Biblical quotations closing with a verse. "Amos Cabot, rest in peace/ Now your mortal trials have ceased. . . ." The church was full. Mr. Cabot had been an outstanding member of the community. He had once run for governor. For a month or so, during his campaign, one saw his picture on barns, walls, buildings, and telephone poles. I don't suppose the sense of walking through a shifting mirror—he found himself at every turn—unsettled him as it would have unsettled me. (Once, for example, when I was in an elevator in Paris I noticed a woman carrying a book of mine. There was a photograph on the jacket and one image of me looked over her arm at another. I wanted the picture, wanted I suppose to destroy it. That she should walk away with my face under her arm seemed to threaten my self-esteem. She left the elevator at the fourth floor and the parting of these two images was confusing. I wanted to follow her, but how could I explain in French—or in any other language—what I felt.) Amos Cabot was not at all like this. He seemed to enjoy seeing himself, and when he lost the election and his face vanished (excepting for a few barns in the back country where it peeled for a month or so) he seemed not perturbed.

There are, of course, the wrong Lowells, the wrong Hallowells, the wrong Eliots, Cheevers, Codmans, and Englishes but today we will deal with the wrong Cabots. Amos came from the South Shore and may never have heard of the North Shore branch of the family. His father had been an auctioneer, which meant in those days an entertainer, horse trader, and sometime crook. Amos owned real estate, the hardware store, the public utilities, and was a director of the bank. He had an office in the Cartwright Block, opposite the green. His wife came from Connecticut, which was, for us at that time, a distant wilderness on whose eastern borders stood the City of New York. New York was populated by harried, nervous, avaricious foreigners who lacked the character to bathe in cold water at six in the morning and to live, with composure, lives of grueling boredom. Mrs. Cabot, when I knew her, was probably in her early forties. She was a short woman with the bright red face of an alcoholic although she was a vigorous temperance worker. Her hair was as white as snow. Her back and her front were prominent and there was a memorable curve to her spine that could have been a cruel corset or the beginnings of lordosis. No one quite knew why Mr. Cabot had married this eccentric from faraway Connecticut—it was, after all, no one's business—but she did own most of the frame tenements on the

East Bank of the river where the workers in the table silver factory lived. Her tenements were profitable but it would have been an unwarranted simplification to conclude that he had married for real estate. She collected the rents herself. I expect that she did her own housework, and she dressed simply, but she wore on her right hand seven large diamond rings. She had evidently read somewhere that diamonds were a sound investment and the blazing stones were about as glamorous as a passbook. There were round diamonds, square diamonds, rectangular diamonds, and some of those diamonds that are set in prongs. On Thursday morning she would wash her diamonds in some jewelers' solution and hang them out to dry in the clothes yard. She never explained this, but the incidence of eccentricity in the village ran so high that her conduct was not thought unusual.

Mrs. Cabot spoke once or twice a year at the St. Botolphs Academy, where many of us went to school. She had three subjects: My Trip to Alaska (slides), The Evils of Drink, and The Evils of Tobacco. Drink was for her so unthinkable a vice that she could not attack it with much vehemence, but the thought of tobacco made her choleric. Could one imagine Christ on the Cross, smoking a cigarette, she would ask us. Could one imagine the Virgin Mary *smoking?* A drop of nicotine fed to a pig by trained laboratory technicians had killed the beast. Etc. She made smoking irresistible, and if I die of lung cancer I shall blame Mrs. Cabot. These performances took place in what we called the Great Study Hall. This was a large room on the second floor that could hold us all. The academy had been built in the 1850s and had the lofty, spacious, and beautiful windows of that period in American architecture. In the spring and in the autumn the building seemed gracefully suspended in its grounds but in the winter a glacial cold fell off the large window lights. In the Great Study Hall we were allowed to wear coats, hats, and gloves. This situation was heightened by the fact that my Great-aunt Anna had bought in Athens a large collection of plaster casts so that we shivered and memorized the donative verbs in the company of at least a dozen buck-naked gods and goddesses. So it was to Hermes and Venus as well as to us that Mrs. Cabot railed against the poisons of tobacco. She was a woman of vehement and ugly prejudice, and I suppose she would have been happy to include the blacks and the Jews but there was only one black and one Jewish family in the village and they were exemplary. The possibility of intolerance in the village did not occur to me until much later, when my mother came to our house in West-chester for Thanksgiving.

This was some years ago, when the New England high-ways had not been completed and the trip from New York or Westchester took over four hours. I left quite early in the morning and drove first to Haverhill, where I stopped at Miss Peacock's School and picked up my niece. I then went on to St. Botolphs, where I found Mother sitting in the hallway in an acolyte's chair. The chair had a steepled back, topped with a wooden fleur-de-lis. From what rain-damp church had this object been stolen? She wore a coat and her bag was at her feet. "I'm ready," she said. She must have been ready for a week. She seemed terribly lonely. "Would you like a drink?" she asked. I knew enough not to take this bait. Had I said yes she would have gone into the pantry and returned, smiling sadly, to say: "Your brother has drunk all the whiskey." So we started back for Westchester. It was a cold, overcast day and I found the drive tiring, although I think fatigue had nothing to do with what followed. I left my niece at my brother's house in Connecticut and drove on to my place. It was after dark when the trip ended. My wife had made all the preparations that were customary for Mother's arrival. There was an open fire, a vase of roses on the piano, and tea with anchovy-paste sandwiches. "How lovely to have flowers," said Mother. "I so love flowers. I can't live without them. Should I suffer some financial reverses and have to choose between flowers and groceries I believe I would choose flowers. . . ."

I do not want to give the impression of an elegant old lady because there were lapses in her performance. I bring up, with powerful unwillingness, a fact that was told to me by her sister after Mother's death. It seems that at one time she applied for a position with the Boston Police Force. She had plenty of money at the time and I have no idea of why she did this. I suppose that she wanted to be a policewoman. I don't know what branch of the force she planned to join, but I've always imagined her in a dark-blue uniform with a ring of keys at her waist and a billy club in her right hand. My grandmother dissuaded her from this course, but the image of a policewoman was some part of the figure she cut, sipping tea by our fire. She meant this evening to be what she called Aristocratic. In this connection she often said: "There must be at least a drop of plebeian blood in the family. How else can one account for your taste in torn and shabby clothing. You've always had plenty of clothes but you've always chosen rags."

I mixed a drink and said how much I had enjoyed seeing my niece.

"Miss Peacock's has changed," Mother said sadly.

"I didn't know," I said. "What do you mean?"

"They've let down the bars."

"I don't understand."

"They're letting in Jews," she said. She fired out the last word.

"Can we change the subject?" I asked.

"I don't see why," she said. "You brought it up."

"My wife is Jewish, Mother," I said. My wife was in the kitchen.

"That is not possible," my mother said. "Her father is Italian."

"Her father," I said, "is a Polish Jew."

"Well," Mother said, "I come from old Massachusetts stock and I'm not ashamed of it although I don't like being called a Yankee."

"There's a difference."

"Your father said that the only good Jew was a dead Jew although I did think Justice Brandeis charming."

"I think it's going to rain," I said. It was one of our staple conversational switch-offs, used to express anger, hunger, love, and the fear of death. My wife joined us and Mother picked up the routine. "It's nearly cold enough for snow," she said. "When you were a boy you used to pray for snow or ice. It depended upon whether you wanted to skate or ski. You were very particular. You would kneel by your bed and loudly ask God to manipulate the elements. You never prayed for anything else. I never once heard you ask for a blessing on your parents. In the summer you didn't pray at all."

The Cabots had two daughters—Geneva and Molly. Geneva was the older and thought to be the more beautiful. Molly was my girl for a year or so. She was a lovely young woman with a sleepy look that was quickly dispelled by a brilliant smile. Her hair was pale brown and held the light. When she was tired or excited sweat formed on her upper lip. In the evenings I would walk to their house and sit with her in the parlor under the most intense surveillance. Mrs. Cabot, of course, regarded sex with utter panic. She watched us from the dining room. From upstairs there were loud and regular thumping sounds. This was Amos Cabot's rowing machine. We were sometimes allowed to take walks together if we kept to the main streets, and when I was old enough to drive I took her to the dances at the club. I was intensely—morbidly—jealous and when she seemed to be enjoying herself with someone else I would stand in the corner, thinking of suicide. I remember driving her back one night to the house on Shore Road.

At the turn of the century someone decided that St. Botolphs might have a future as a resort, and five mansions, or follies, were built at the end of Shore Road. The Cabots lived in one of these. All the mansions had towers. These were round with conical roofs, rising a story or so above the rest of the frame buildings. The towers were strikingly unmilitary, and so I suppose they were meant to express romance. What did they contain? Dens, I guess, maids' rooms, broken furniture, trunks, and they must have been the favorite of hornets. I parked my car in front of the Cabots' and turned off the lights. The house above us was dark.

It was long ago, so long ago that the foliage of elm trees was part of the summer night. (It was so long ago that when you wanted to make a left turn you cranked down the car window and *pointed* in that direction. Otherwise you were not allowed to point. Don't point, you were told. I can't imagine why, unless the gesture was thought to be erotic.) The dances —the Assemblies—were formal and I would be wearing a tuxedo handed down from my father to my brother and from my brother to me like some escutcheon or sumptuary torch. I took Molly in my arms. She was completely responsive. I am not a tall man (I am sometimes inclined to stoop), but the conviction that I am loved and loving affects me like a military bracing. Up goes my head. My back is straight. I am six foot seven and sustained by some clamorous emotional uproar. Sometimes my ears ring. It can happen anywhere—in a ginseng house in Seoul, for example—but it happened that night in front of the Cabots' house on Shore Road. Molly said then that she had to go. Her mother would be watching from a window. She asked me not to come up to the house. I mustn't have heard. I went with her up the walk and the stairs to the porch, where she tried the door and found it locked. She asked me again to go, but I couldn't abandon her there, could I? Then a light went on and the door was opened by a dwarf. He was exhaustively misshapen. The head was hydrocephalic, the features were swollen, the legs were thick and cruelly bowed. I thought of the circus. The lovely young woman began to cry. She stepped into the house and closed the door and I was left with the summer night, the elms, the taste of an east wind. After this she avoided me for a week or so and I was told the facts by Maggie, our old cook.

But more facts first. It was in the summer, and in the summer most of us went to a camp on the Cape run by the headmaster of the St. Botolphs Academy. The months were so feckless, so blue, that I can't remember them at all. I slept next to a boy named DeVarrenes whom I had known all my life. We were together most of the time. We played marbles together, slept together, played together on the same backfield, and once to-gether took a ten-day canoe trip during which we nearly drowned together. My brother claimed that we had begun to look alike. It was the most gratifying and unself-conscious rela-tionship I had known. (He still calls me once or twice a year from San Francisco, where he lives unhappily with his wife and three unmarried daughters. He sounds drunk. "We were happy, weren't we," he asks.) One day another boy, a stranger named Wallace, asked if I wanted to swim across the lake. I might claim that I knew nothing about Wallace, and I knew very little, but I did know or sense that he was lonely. It was as conspicuous as—or more conspicuous than—any of his features. He did what was expected of him. He played ball, made his bed, took sailing lessons, and got his life-saving certificate, but this seemed more like a careful imposture than any sort of participation. He was miserable, he was lonely, and sooner or later, rain or shine, he would say so and, in the act of confession, make an impossible claim on one's loyalty. One knew all of this but one pretended not to. We got a permission from the swimming instructor and swam across the lake. We used a clumsy sidestroke that still seems to me more serviceable than the overhand that is obligatory these days in those swimming pools where I spend most of my time. The sidestroke is Lower Class. I've seen it once in a swimming pool, and when I asked who the swimmer was I was told he was the butler. When the ship sinks, when the plane ditches I will try to reach the life raft with an overhand and drown stylishly, whereas if I had used a Lower-Class sidestroke I would have lived forever.

We swam the lake, rested in the sun—no confidences—and swam home. When I came up to our cabin DeVarennes took me aside. "Don't ever let me see you with Wallace again," he said. I asked why. He told me. "Wallace is Amos Cabot's bastard. His mother is a whore. They live in one of the tenements across the river."

The next day was hot and brilliant and Wallace asked if I wanted to swim the lake again. I said sure, sure and we did. When we came back to camp DeVarennes wouldn't speak to me. That night a northeaster blew up and it rained for three days. DeVarennes seems to have forgiven me and I don't re-

call having crossed the lake with Wallace again. As for the
dwarf, Maggie told me he was a son of Mrs. Cabot from an
earlier marriage. He worked at the table silver factory but he
went to work early in the morning and didn't return until after
dark. His existence was meant to be kept a secret. This was
unusual but not—at the time of which I'm writing—unprecedented. The Trumbulls kept Mrs. Trumbull's crazy sister
hidden in the attic and Uncle Peepee Marshmallow—an exhi-
bitionist—was often hidden for months.

It was a winter afternoon, an early winter afternoon. Mrs.
Cabot washed her diamonds and hung them out to dry. She
then went upstairs to take a nap. She claimed that she had never
taken a nap in her life, and the sounder she slept the more
vehement were her claims that she didn't sleep. This was not
so much an eccentricity on her part as it was a crabwise way
of presenting the facts that was prevalent in that part of the
world. She woke at four and went down to gather her stones.
They were gone. She called Geneva, but there was no answer.
She got a rake and scored the stubble under the clothesline.
There was nothing. She called the police.

As I say, it was a winter afternoon and the winters there
were very cold. We counted for heat—sometimes for survival
—on wood fires and large coal-burning furnaces that sometimes got out of hand. A winter night was a threatening fact,
and this may have partly accounted for the sentiment with
which we watched—in late November and December—the
light burn out in the west. (My father's journals, for example,
were full of descriptions of winter twilights, not because he
was at all crepuscular but because the coming of the night
might mean danger and pain.) Geneva had packed a bag, gathered the diamonds, and taken the last train out of town: the
4:37. How thrilling it must have been. The diamonds were

meant to be stolen. They were a flagrant snare and she did what she was meant to do. She took a train to New York that night and sailed three days later for Alexandria on a Cunarder—the S.S. *Serapis*. She took a boat from Alexandria to Luxor, where, in the space of two months, she joined the Moslem faith and married an Egyptian noble.

I read about the theft next day in the evening paper. I delivered papers. I had begun my route on foot, moved on to a bicycle, and was assigned, when I was sixteen, to an old Ford truck. I was a truck driver! I hung around the linotype room until the papers were printed and then drove around to the four neighboring villages, tossing out bundles at the doors of the candy and stationery stores. During the World Series a second edition with box scores was brought out, and after dark I would make the trip again to Travertine and the other places along the shore. The roads were dark, there was very little traffic, and leaf-burning had not been forbidden so that the air was tannic, melancholy, and exciting. One can attach a mysterious and inordinate amount of importance to some simple journey, and this second trip with the box scores made me very happy. I dreaded the end of the World Series as one dreads the end of any pleasure, and had I been younger I would have prayed. CABOT JEWELS STOLEN was the headline and the incident was never again mentioned in the paper. It was not mentioned at all in our house, but this was not unusual. When Mr. Abbott hung himself from the pear tree next door this was never mentioned.

Molly and I took a walk on the beach at Travertine that Sunday afternoon. I was troubled, but Molly's troubles were much graver. It did not disturb her that Geneva had stolen the diamonds. She only wanted to know what had become of her sister, and she was not to find out for another six weeks. However, something had happened at the house that night. There had been a scene between her parents and her father had left. She described this to me. We were walking barefoot. She was crying. I would like to have forgotten the scene as soon as she finished her description.

Children drown, beautiful women are mangled in automobile accidents, cruise ships founder, and men die lingering deaths in mines and submarines, but you will find none of this in my accounts. In the last chapter the ship comes home to port, the children are saved, the miners will be rescued. Is this an infirmity of the genteel or a conviction that there are discernible moral truths? Mr. X defecated in his wife's top drawer. This is a fact, but I claim that it is not a truth. In describing St. Botolphs I would sooner stay on the West Bank of the river where the houses were white and where the church bells rang, but over the bridge there was the table silver factory, the tenements (owned by Mrs. Cabot), and the Commercial Hotel. At low tide one could smell the sea gas from the inlets at Travertine. The headlines in the afternoon paper dealt with a trunk murder. The women on the streets were ugly. Even the dummies in the one store window seemed stooped, depressed, and dressed in clothing that neither fitted nor became them. Even the bride in her splendor seemed to have got some bad news. The politics were neofascist, the factory was nonunion, the food was unpalatable, and the night wind was bitter. This was a provincial and a traditional world enjoying few of the rewards of smallness and traditionalism, and when I speak of the blessedness of all small places I speak of the West Bank. On the East Bank was the Commercial Hotel, the demesne of Doris, a male prostitute who worked as a supervisor in the factory during the day and hustled the bar at night, exploiting the extraordinary moral lassitude of the place. Everybody knew

Doris, and many of the customers had used him at one time or another. There was no scandal and no delight involved. Doris would charge a traveling salesman whatever he could get but he did it with the regulars for nothing. This seemed less like tolerance than hapless indifference, the absence of vision, moral stamina, the splendid Ambitiousness of romantic love. On fight night Doris drifts down the bar. Buy him a drink and he'll put his hand on your arm, your shoulder, your waist, and move a fraction of an inch in his direction and he'll reach for the cake. The steam fitter buys him a drink, the high school dropout, the watch repairman. (Once a stranger shouted to the bartender: "Tell that sonofabitch to take his tongue out of my ear" —but he was a stranger.) This is not a transient world, these are not drifters, more than half of these men will never live in any other place, and yet this seems to be the essence of spiritual nomadism. The telephone rings and the bartender beckons to Doris. There's a customer in room eight. Why would I sooner be on the West Shore where my parents are playing bridge with Mr. and Mrs. Eliot Pinkham in the golden light of a great gas chandelier?

I'll blame it on the roast, the roast, the Sunday roast bought from a butcher who wore a straw boater with a pheasant wing in the hat band. I suppose the roast entered our house, wrapped in bloody paper on Thursday or Friday, traveling on the back of a bicycle. It would be a gross exaggeration to say that the meat had the detonative force of a land mine that could savage your eyes and your genitals but its powers were disproportionate. We sat down to dinner after church. (My brother was living in Omaha so we were only three.) My father would hone the carving knife and make a cut in the meat. My father was very adroit with an ax and a crosscut saw and could bring down a large tree with dispatch, but the Sunday roast was something else. After he had made the first cut my mother would sigh. This was an extraordinary performance so loud, so profound, that it seemed as if her life were in danger. It seemed as if her very soul might come unhinged and drift out of her open mouth. "Will you never learn, Leander, that lamb must be carved against the grain?" she would ask. Once the battle of the roast had begun the exchanges were so swift, predictable, and tedious that there would be no point in reporting them. After five or six wounding remarks my father would wave the carving knife in the air and shout: "Will you kindly mind your own business, will you kindly shut up?" She would sigh once more and put her hand to her heart. Surely this was her last breath. Then, studying the air above the table she would say: "Feel that refreshing breeze."

There was, of course, seldom a breeze. It could be airless, midwinter, rainy, anything. The remark was one for all seasons. Was it a commendable metaphor for hope, for the serenity of love (which I think she had never experienced), was it nostalgia for some summer evening when, loving and understanding, we sat contentedly on the lawn above the river? Was it no better or no worse than the sort of smile thrown at the evening star by a man who is in utter despair? Was it a prophecy of that generation to come who would be so drilled in evasiveness that they would be denied forever the splendors of a passionate confrontation?

The scene changes to Rome. It is spring when the canny swallows flock into the city to avoid the wingshots in Ostia. The noise the birds make seems like light as the light of day loses its brilliance. Then one hears, across the courtyard, the voice of an American woman. She is screaming. "You're a goddamned fucked-up no-good insane piece of shit. You can't make a nickel, you don't have a friend in the world, and in bed

you stink. . . ." There is no reply, and one wonders if she is
railing at the dark. Then you hear a man cough. That's all you
will hear from him. "Oh, I know I've lived with you for eight
years, but if you ever thought I liked it, any of it, it's only because you're such a chump you wouldn't know the real thing
if you had it. When I really come the pictures *fall* off the walls.
With you it's always an act. . . ." The highlow bells that ring
in Rome at that time of day have begun to chime. I smile at
this sound although it has no bearing on my life, my faith, no
true harmony, nothing like the revelations in the voice across
the court. Why would I sooner describe church bells and flocks
of swallows? Is this puerile, a sort of greeting-card mentality,
a whimsical and effeminate refusal to look at facts? On and on
she goes but I will follow her no longer. She attacks his hair,
his brain, and his spirit while I observe that a light rain has begun to fall and that the effect of this is to louden the noise of
traffic on the Corso. Now she is hysterical—her voice is break-
ing—and I think perhaps that at the height of her malediction
she will begin to cry and ask his forgiveness. She will not, of
course. She will go after him with a carving knife and he will
end up in the emergency ward of the Policlinico, claiming to
have wounded himself, but as I go out for dinner, smiling at
beggars, fountains, children, and the first stars of evening, I as-
sure myself that everything will work out for the best. Feel
that refreshing breeze.

My recollections of the Cabots are only a footnote to my
principal work and I go to work early these winter mornings.
It is still dark. Here and there, standing on street corners, waiting for buses, are women dressed in white. They wear white
shoes, white stockings, and white uniforms can be seen below
their winter coats. Are they nurses, beauty parlor operators,
dentists' helpers? I'll never know. They usually carry a brown

paper bag holding, I guess, a ham on rye and a Thermos of buttermilk. Traffic is light at this time of day. A laundry truck delivers uniforms to the Fried Chicken Shack and in Asburn Place there is a milk truck—the last of that generation. It will be half an hour before the yellow school buses start their rounds.

I work in an apartment house called the Prestwick. It is seven stories high and dates, I guess, from the late twenties. It is of a Tudor persuasion. The bricks are irregular, there is a parapet on the roof, and the sign advertising vacancies is literally a shingle that hangs from iron chains and creaks romantically in the wind. On the right of the door there is a list of perhaps twenty-five doctors' names, but these are not gentle healers with stethoscopes and rubber hammers, these are psychiatrists, and this is the country of the plastic chair and the full ashtray. I don't know why they should have chosen this place, but they outnumber the other tenants. Now and then you see, waiting for the elevator, a woman with a grocery wagon and a child, but you mostly see the sometimes harried faces of men and women with trouble. They sometimes smile; they sometimes talk to themselves. Business seems slow these days, and the doctor whose office is next to mine often stands in the hallway, staring out of the window. What does a psychiatrist think? Does he wonder what has become of those patients who gave up, who refused Group Therapy, who disregarded his warnings and admonitions? He will know their secrets. I tried to murder my husband. I tried to murder my wife. Three years ago I took an overdose of sleeping pills. The year before that I cut my wrists. My mother wanted me to be a girl. My mother wanted me to be a boy. My mother wanted me to be a homosexual. Where had they gone, what were they doing? Were they still married, quarreling at the dinner table, decorating the Christmas tree? Had they divorced, remarried, jumped off bridges, taken Seconal, struck some kind of truce, turned homosexual, or moved to a farm in Vermont where they planned to raise strawberries and lead a simple life? The doctor sometimes stands by the window for an hour.

My real work these days is to write an edition of *The New York Times* that will bring gladness to the hearts of men. How better could I occupy myself? The *Times* is a critical if rusty link in my ties to reality, but in these last years its tidings have been monotonous. The prophets of doom are out of work. All one can do is to pick up the pieces. The lead story is this: PRESIDENT'S HEART TRANSPLANT DEEMED SUCCESSFUL. There is this box on the lower left: COST OF J. EDGAR HOOVER MEMORIAL CHALLENGED. "The subcommittee on memorials threatened today to halve the seven million dollars appropriated to commemorate the late J. Edgar Hoover with a Temple of Justice. . . ." Column three: CONTROVERSIAL LEGISLATION REPEALED BY SENATE. "The recently enacted bill, making it a felony to have wicked thoughts about the administration, was repealed this afternoon by a standup vote of forty-three to seven." On and on it goes. There are robust and heartening editorials, thrilling sports news, and the weather of course is always sunny and warm unless we need rain. Then we have rain. The air pollutant gradient is zero, and even in Tokyo fewer and fewer people are wearing surgical masks. All highways, throughways, and expressways will be closed for the holiday weekend. Joy to the World!

But to get back to the Cabots. The scene that I would like to overlook or forget took place the night after Geneva had stolen the diamonds. It involves plumbing. Most of the houses

29

in the village had relatively little plumbing. There was usually a water closet in the basement for the cook and the ash man and a single bathroom on the second floor for the rest of the household. Some of these rooms were quite large, and the Endicotts had a fireplace in their bathroom. Somewhere along the line Mrs. Cabot decided that the bathroom was her demesne. She had a locksmith come and secure the door. Mr. Cabot was allowed to take his sponge bath every morning, but after this the bathroom door was locked and Mrs. Cabot kept the key in her pocket. Mr. Cabot was obliged to use a chamber pot, but since he came from the South Shore I don't suppose this was much of a hardship. It may even have been nostalgic. He was using the chamber pot late that night when Mrs. Cabot came to the door of his room. (They slept in separate rooms.) "Will you close the door?" she screamed. "Will you close the door? Do I have to listen to that horrible noise for the rest of my life?" They would both be in nightgowns, her snow-white hair in braids. She picked up the chamber pot and threw its contents at him. He kicked down the door of the locked bathroom, washed, dressed, packed a bag, and walked over the bridge to Mrs. Wallace's place on the East Bank.

He stayed there for three days and then returned. He was worried about Molly, and in such a small place there were appearances to be considered—Mrs. Wallace's as well as his own. He divided his time between the East and the West banks of the river until a week or so later, when he was taken ill. He felt languid. He stayed in bed until noon. When he dressed and went to his office he returned after an hour or so. The doctor examined him and found nothing wrong.

One evening Mrs. Wallace saw Mrs. Cabot coming out of the drugstore on the East Bank. She watched her rival cross the bridge and then went into the drugstore and asked the clerk if Mrs. Cabot was a regular customer. "I've been wondering about that myself," the clerk said. "Of course she comes over here to collect her rents, but I always thought she used the other drugstore. She comes in here to buy ant poison—arsenic, that is. She says they have these terrible ants in the house on Shore Road and arsenic is the only way of getting rid of them. From the way she buys arsenic the ants must be terrible." Mrs. Wallace might have warned Mr. Cabot but she never saw him again.

She went after the funeral to Judge Simmons and said that she wanted to charge Mrs. Cabot with murder. The drug clerk would have a record of her purchase of arsenic that would be incriminating. "He may have them," the judge said, "but he won't give them to you. What you are asking for is an exhumation of the body and a long trial in Barnstable, and you have neither the money nor the reputation to support this. You were his friend, I know, for sixteen years. He was a splendid man and why don't you console yourself with the thought of how many years it was that you knew him? And another thing. He's left you and Wallace a substantial legacy. If Mrs. Cabot were provoked to contest the will you could lose this."

I went out to Luxor to see Geneva. I flew to London in a 747. There were only three passengers; but as I say the prophets of doom are out of work. I went from Cairo up the Nile in a low-flying two-motor prop. The sameness of wind erosion and water erosion makes the Sahara there seem to have been gutted by floods, rivers, courses, streams, and brooks, the thrust of a natural search. The scorings are watery and arboreal, and as a false stream bed spreads out it takes the shape of a tree, striving for light. It was freezing in Cairo when we left before dawn. Luxor, where Geneva met me at the airport, was hot.

I was very happy to see her, so happy I was unobservant, but I did notice that she had gotten fat. I don't mean that she was heavy; I mean that she weighed about three hundred pounds. She was a fat woman. Her hair, once a coarse yellow, was now golden but her Massachusetts accent was as strong as ever. It sounded like music to me on the Upper Nile. Her husband—now a colonel—was a slender, middle-aged man, a relative of the last king. He owned a restaurant at the edge of the city and they lived in a pleasant apartment over the dining room. The colonel was humorous, intelligent—a rake, I guess —and a heavy drinker. When we went to the temple at Karnak our dragoman carried ice, tonic, and gin. I spent a week with them, mostly in temples and graves. We spent the evenings in his bar. War was threatening—the air was full of Russian planes—and the only other tourist was an Englishman who sat at the bar, reading his passport. On the last day I swam in the Nile—overhand—and they drove me to the airport, where I kissed Geneva—and the Cabots—good-bye.

 *Percy*

Reminiscence, along with the cheese boards and ugly pottery sometimes given to brides, seems to have a manifest destiny with the sea. Reminiscences are written on such a table as this, corrected, published, read, and then they begin their inevitable journey toward the bookshelves in those houses and cottages one rents for the summer. In the last house we rented, we had beside our bed the *Memories of a Grand Duchess,* the *Recollections of a Yankee Whaler,* and a paperback copy of *Goodbye to All That,* but it is the same all over the world. The only book in my hotel room in Taormina was *Recordi d'un Soldato Garibaldino,* and in my room in Yalta I found «Повесть о Жизни.» Unpopularity is surely some part of this drifting toward salt water, but since the sea is our most universal symbol for memory, might there not be some mysterious affinity between these published recollections and the thunder of waves? So I put down what follows with the happy conviction that these pages will find their way into some bookshelf with a good view of a stormy coast. I can even see the room—see the straw rug, the window glass clouded with salt, and feel the house shake to the ringing of a heavy sea.

Great-uncle Ebenezer was stoned on the streets of Newburyport for his abolitionist opinions. His demure wife, Georgiana (an artiste on the pianoforte), used once or twice a month to braid feathers into her hair, squat on the floor, light a pipe, and, having been given by psychic forces the personality of an Indian squaw, receive messages from the dead. My father's cousin, Anna Boynton, who had taught Greek at Radcliffe, starved herself to death during the Armenian famine. She and her sister Nanny had the copper skin, high cheekbones, and black hair of the Natick Indians. My father liked to recall the night he drank all the champagne on the New York–Boston train. He started drinking splits with some friend before dinner, and when they finished the splits they emptied the quarts and the magnums and were working on a jeroboam when the train reached Boston. He felt that this guzzling was heroic. My Uncle Hamlet—a black-mouthed old wreck who had starred on the Newburyport Volunteer Fire Department ball team—called me to the side of his deathbed and shouted, "I've had the best fifty years of this country's history. *You* can have the rest." He seemed to hand it to me on a platter—droughts, depressions, convulsions of nature, pestilence, and war. He was wrong, of course, but the idea pleased him. This all took place in the environs of Athenian Boston, but the family seemed much closer to the hyperbole and rhetoric that stem from Wales, Dublin, and the various principalities of alcohol than to the sermons of Phillips Brooks.

One of the most vivid members of my mother's side of the family was an aunt who called herself Percy, and who smoked cigars. There was no sexual ambiguity involved. She was lovely, fair, and intensely feminine. We were never very close. My father may have disliked her, although I don't recall this. My maternal grandparents had emigrated from England in the 1890s with their six children. My Grandfather Holinshed was described as a bounder—a word that has always evoked for me the image of a man leaping over a hedge just ahead of a charge of buckshot. I don't know what mistakes he had made in England, but his transportation to the New World was financed by his father-in-law, Sir Percy Devere, and he was paid a small remittance so long as he did not return to England. He detested the United States and died a few years after his arrival here. On the day of his funeral, Grandmother announced to her children that there would be a family conference in the evening. They should be prepared to discuss their plans. When the conference was called, Grandmother asked the children in turn what they planned to make of their lives. Uncle Tom wanted to be a soldier. Uncle Harry wanted to be a sailor. Uncle Bill wanted to be a merchant. Aunt Emily wanted to marry. Mother wanted to be a nurse and heal the sick. Aunt Florence—who later called herself Percy—exclaimed, "I wish to be a great painter, like the Masters of the Italian Renaissance!" Grandmother then said, "Since at least one of you has a clear idea of her destiny, the rest of you will go to work and Florence will go to art school." That is what they did, and so far as I know none of them ever resented this decision.

How smooth it all seems and how different it must have been. The table where they gathered would have been lighted by whale oil or kerosene. They lived in a farmhouse in Dorchester. They would have had lentils or porridge or at best stew for dinner. They were very poor. If it was in the winter, they would be cold, and after the conference the wind would extinguish Grandmother's candle—stately Grandmother—as she went down the back path to the malodorous outhouse. They couldn't have bathed more than once a week, and I suppose they bathed out of pails. The succinctness of Percy's exclamation seems to have obscured the facts of a destitute widow with six children. Someone must have washed all those dishes, and washed them in greasy water, drawn from a pump and heated over a fire.

The threat of gentility in such recollections is Damoclean, but these were people without pretense or affectation, and when Grandmother spoke French at the dinner table, as she often did, she merely meant to put her education to some practical use. It was, of course, a much simpler world. For example, Grandmother read in the paper one day that a drunken butcher, the father of four, had chopped up his wife with a meat cleaver, and she went directly to Boston by horsecar or hansom—whatever transportation was available. There was a crowd around the tenement where the murder had taken place, and two policemen guarded the door. Grandmother got past the policemen and found the butcher's four terrified children in a bloody apartment. She got their clothes together, took the children home with her, and kept them for a month or longer, when other homes were found. Cousin Anna's decision to starve and Percy's wish to become a painter were made with the same directness. It was what Percy thought she could do best—what would make most sense of her life.

She began to call herself Percy in art school, because she felt that there was some prejudice against women in the arts. In her last year in art school she did a six-by-fourteen-foot painting of Orpheus taming the beasts. This won her a gold medal and a trip to Europe, where she studied at the Beaux-Arts for a few months. When she returned, she was given three portrait commissions, but she was much too skeptical to succeed at this. Her portraits were pictorial indictments, and all three of them were unacceptable. She was not an aggressive woman, but she was immoderate and critical.

After her return from France she met a young doctor named Abbott Tracy at some yacht club on the North Shore. I don't mean the Corinthian. I mean some briny huddle of driftwood nailed together by weekend sailors. Moths in the billiard felt. Salvaged furniture. Two earth closets labeled "Ladies" and "Gentlemen," and moorings for a dozen of those wide-waisted catboats that my father used to say sailed like real estate. Percy and Abbott Tracy met in some such place, and she fell in love. He had already begun a formidable and clinical sexual career, and seemed unacquainted in any way with sentiment, although I recall that he liked to watch children saying their prayers. Percy listened for his footsteps, she languished in his absence, his cigar cough sounded to her like music, and she filled a portfolio with pencil sketches of his face, his eyes, his hands, and, after their marriage, the rest of him.

They bought an old house in West Roxbury. The ceilings were low, the rooms were dark, the windows were small, and the fireplaces smoked. Percy liked all of this, and shared with my mother a taste for drafty ruins that seemed odd in such high-minded women. She turned a spare bedroom into a studio and did another large canvas—Prometheus bringing fire to man. This was exhibited in Boston, but no one bought it. She then painted a nymph and centaur. This used to be in the attic, and the centaur looked exactly like Uncle Abbott. Uncle Abbott's practice was not very profitable, and I guess he was lazy. I remember seeing him eating his breakfast in pajamas at one in the afternoon. They must have been poor, and I suppose Percy did the housework, bought the groceries, and hung out the wash. Late one night when I had gone to bed, I overheard my father shouting, "I cannot support that cigar-smoking sister of yours any longer." Percy spent some time copying paintings at Fenway Court. This brought in a little money, but evidently not enough. One of her friends from art school urged her to try painting magazine covers. This went deeply against all of her aspirations and instincts, but it must have seemed to her that she had no choice, and she began to turn out deliberately sentimental pictures for magazines. She got to be quite famous at this.

She was never pretentious, but she couldn't forget that she had not explored to the best of her ability those gifts that she may have had, and her enthusiasm for painting was genuine. When she was able to employ a cook, she gave the cook painting lessons. I remember her saying, toward the end of her life, "Before I die, I must go back to the Boston Museum and see the Sargent watercolors." When I was sixteen or seventeen, I took a walking tour in Germany with my brother and bought Percy some van Gogh reproductions in Munich. She was very excited by these. Painting, she felt, had some organic vitality— it was the exploration of continents of consciousness, and here was a new world. The deliberate puerility of most of her work had damaged her draftsmanship, and at one point she began to hire a model on Saturday mornings and sketch from life. Going there on some simple errand—the return of a book or a newspaper clipping—I stepped into her studio and found, sitting on the floor, a naked young woman. "Nellie Casey," said Percy, "this is my nephew, Ralph Warren." She went on sketching. The model smiled sweetly—it was nearly a social smile and seemed to partially temper her monumental nakedness. Her breasts were very beautiful, and the nipples, relaxed and faintly colored, were bigger than silver dollars. The atmosphere was not erotic or playful, and I soon left. I dreamed for years of Nellie Casey. Percy's covers brought in enough money for her to buy a house on the Cape, a house in Maine, a large automobile, and a small painting by Whistler that used to hang in the living room beside a copy Percy had made of Titian's *Europa*.

Her first son, Lovell, was born in the third year of her marriage. When he was four or five years old, it was decided that he was a musical genius, and he did have unusual manual dexterity. He was great at unsnarling kite lines and fishing tackle. He was taken out of school, educated by tutors, and spent most of his time practicing the piano. I detested him for a number of reasons. He was extremely dirty-minded, and used oil on his hair. My brother and I wouldn't have been more disconcerted if he had crowned himself with flowers. He not only used oil in his hair but when he came to visit us he left the hair-oil bottle in our medicine cabinet. He had his first recital in Steinway Hall when he was eight or nine, and he always played a Beethoven sonata when the family got together.

Percy must have perceived, early in her marriage, that her husband's lechery was compulsive and incurable, but she was determined, like any other lover, to authenticate her suspicion. How could a man that she adored be faithless? She hired a detective agency, which tracked him down to an apartment house near the railroad station called the Orpheus. Percy went there and found him in bed with an unemployed telephone operator. He was smoking a cigar and drinking whiskey. "Now, Percy," he is supposed to have said, "why did you have to go and do this?" She then came to our house and stayed with us for a week or so. She was pregnant, and when her son Beaufort was born his brain or his nervous system was seriously damaged. Abbott always claimed that there was nothing wrong with his

son, but when Beaufort was five or six years old he was sent off
to some school or institution in Connecticut. He used to come
home for the holidays, and had learned to sit through an adult
meal, but that was about all. He was an arsonist, and he once
exposed himself at an upstairs window while Lovell was playing the "Waldstein." In spite of all this, Percy was never bitter
or melancholy, and continued to worship Uncle Abbott.

The family used to gather, as I recall, almost every Sunday.
I don't know why they should have spent so much time in one
another's company. Perhaps they had few friends or perhaps
they held their family ties above friendship. Standing in the
rain outside the door of Percy's old house, we seemed bound
together not by blood and not by love but by a sense that the
world and its works were hostile. The house was dark. It had
a liverish smell.

The guests often included Grandmother and old Nanny
Boynton, whose sister had starved herself to death. Nanny
taught music in the Boston public schools until her retirement,
when she moved to a farm on the South Shore. Here she raised
bees and mushrooms, and read musical scores—Puccini,
Mozart, Debussy, Brahms, etc.—that were mailed to her by a
friend in the public library. I remember her very pleasantly.
She looked, as I've said, like a Natick Indian. Her nose was
beaked, and when she went to the beehives she covered herself
with cheesecloth and sang *Vissi d'arte.* I once overheard
someone say that she was drunk a good deal of the time, but I
don't believe it. She stayed with Percy when the winter
weather was bad, and she always traveled with a set of the
Britannica, which was set up in the dining room behind her
chair to settle disputes.

The meals at Percy's were very heavy. When the wind
blew, the fireplaces smoked. Leaves and rain fell outside the

windows. By the time we retired to the dark living room, we were all uncomfortable. Lovell would then be asked to play. The first notes of the Beethoven sonata would transform that dark, close, malodorous room into a landscape of extraordinary beauty. A cottage stood in some green fields near a river. A woman with flaxen hair stepped out of the door and dried her hands on an apron. She called her lover. She called and called, but something was wrong. A storm was approaching. The river would flood. The bridge would be washed away. The bass was massive, gloomy, and prophetic. Beware, beware! Traffic casualties were unprecedented. Storms lashed the west coast of Florida. Pittsburgh was paralyzed by a blackout. Famine gripped Philadelphia, and there was no hope for anyone. Then the lyric treble sang a long song about love and beauty. When this was done, down came the bass again, fortified by more bad news reports. The storm was traveling north through Georgia and Virginia. Traffic casualties were mounting. There was cholera in Nebraska. The Mississippi was over its banks. A live volcano had erupted in the Appalachians. Alas, alas! The treble resumed its part of the argument, persuasive, hopeful, purer than any human voice I had ever heard. Then the two voices began their counterpoint, and on it went to the end.

One afternoon, when the music was finished, Lovell, Uncle Abbott, and I got into the car and drove into the Dorchester slums. It was in the early winter, already dark and rainy, and the rains of Boston fell with great authority. He parked the car in front of a frame tenement and said that he was going to see a patient.

"You think he's going to see a patient?" Lovell asked.

"Yes," I said.

"He's going to see his girl friend," Lovell said. Then he began to cry.

I didn't like him. I had no sympathy to give him. I only wished that I had more seemly relations. He dried his tears, and we sat there without speaking until Uncle Abbott returned, whistling, contented, and smelling of perfume. He took us to a drugstore for some ice cream, and then we went back to the house, where Percy was opening the living-room windows to let in some air. She seemed tired but still high-spirited, although I suppose that she and everyone else in the room knew what Abbott had been up to. It was time for us to go home.

Lovell entered the Eastman Conservatory when he was fifteen, and performed the Beethoven G-Major Concerto with the Boston orchestra the year he graduated. Having been drilled never to mention money, it seems strange that I should recall the financial details of his debut. His tails cost one hundred dollars, his coach charged five hundred, and the orchestra paid him three hundred for two performances. The family was scattered throughout the hall, so we were unable to concentrate our excitement, but we were all terribly excited. After the concert we went to the greenroom and drank champagne. Koussevitzky did not appear, but Burgin, the concertmaster, was there. The reviews in the *Herald* and the *Transcript* were fairly complimentary, but they both pointed out that Lovell's playing lacked sentiment. That winter, Lovell and Percy went on a tour that took them as far west as Chicago, and something went wrong. They may, as travelers, have been bad company for one another; he may have had poor notices or small audiences; and while nothing was ever said, I recall that the tour was not triumphant. When they returned, Percy sold a piece of property that adjoined the house and went to Europe for the summer. Lovell could surely have supported himself as a musician, but instead he took a job as a manual laborer for some electrical instrument company. He came to see us before Percy returned, and told me what had been happening that summer.

"Daddy didn't spend much time around the house after Mother went away," he said, "and I was alone most evenings. I used to get my own supper, and I spent a lot of time at the movies. I used to try and pick up girls, but I'm skinny and I don't have much self-confidence. Well, one Sunday I drove down to this beach in the old Buick. Daddy let me have the old Buick. I saw this very fat couple with a young daughter. They looked lonely. Mrs. Hirshman is very fat, and she makes herself up like a clown, and she has a little dog. There is a kind of fat woman who always has a little dog. So then I said something about how I loved dogs, and they seemed happy to talk with me, and then I ran into the waves and showed off my crawl and came back and sat with them. They were Germans, and they had a funny accent, and I think their funny English and their fatness made them lonely. Well, their daughter was named Donna-Mae, and she was all wrapped up in a bathrobe, and she had on a hat, and they told me she had such fair skin she had to keep out of the sun. Then they told me she had beautiful hair, and she took off her hat, and I saw her hair for the first time. It *was* beautiful. It was the color of honey and very long, and her skin was pearly. You could see that the sun would burn it. So we talked, and I got some hot dogs and tonic, and took Donna-Mae for a walk up the beach, and I was very happy. Then, when the day was over, I offered to drive them home—they'd come to the beach in a bus—and they said they'd like a ride if I'd promise to have supper with them. They lived in a sort of a slum, and he was a house painter. Their house was behind another house. Mrs. Hirshman said while she cooked supper why didn't I wash Donna-Mae off with the hose? I remember this very clearly, because it's when I fell in love. She put on her bathing suit again, and I put on my bathing suit, and I sprayed her very gently with the hose. She squealed a little, naturally, because the water was cold, and it was getting dark, and in the house next door someone was playing the Chopin C-Sharp-Minor, Opus 28. The piano was out of tune, and the person didn't know how to play, but the music and the hose and Donna-Mae's pearly skin and golden hair and the smells of supper from the kitchen and the twilight all seemed to be a kind of paradise. So I had supper with them and went home, and the next night I took Donna-Mae to the movies. Then I had supper with them again, and when I told Mrs. Hirshman that my mother was away and that I almost never saw my father, she said that they had a spare room and why didn't I stay there? So the next night I packed some clothes and moved into their spare room, and I've been there ever since."

It is unlikely that Percy would have written my mother after her return from Europe, and, had she written, the letter would have been destroyed, since that family had a crusading detestation of souvenirs. Letters, photographs, diplomas—anything that authenticated the past was always thrown into the fire. I think this was not, as they claimed, a dislike of clutter but a fear of death. To glance backward was to die, and they did not mean to leave a trace. There was no such letter, but had there been one it would, in the light of what I was told, have gone like this:

DEAR POLLY:

Lovell met me at the boat on Thursday. I bought him a Beethoven autograph in Rome, but before I had a chance to give it to him he announced that he was engaged to be married. He can't afford to marry, of course, and when I asked him how he planned to support a family he said that he had a job with some electrical instrument company. When I asked about his music he said he would keep it up in the evenings. I do not want to run his life and I want him to be happy but I could not forget the amount of money that has been poured into his musical education. I had looked forward to coming home and I was very upset to receive this news as soon as I got off the boat. Then he told me that he no longer lived with his father and me. He lives with his future parents-in-law.

I was kept busy getting settled and I had to go into Boston several times to find work so I wasn't able to entertain his fiancée until I had been back a week or two. I asked her for tea. Lovell asked me not to smoke cigars and I agreed to this. I could see his point. He is very uneasy about what he calls my "bohemianism" and I wanted to make a good impression. They came at four. Her name is Donna-Mae Hirshman. Her parents are German immigrants. She is twenty-one years old and works as a clerk in some insurance office. Her voice is high. She giggles. The one thing that can be said in her favor is that she has a striking head of yellow hair. I suppose Lovell may be attracted by her fairness but this hardly seems reason enough to marry. She giggled when we were introduced. She sat on the red sofa and as soon as she saw *Europa* she giggled again. Lovell could not take his eyes off her. I poured her tea and asked if she wanted lemon or cream. She said she didn't know. Then I asked politely what she usually took in her tea and she said she'd never drunk tea before. Then I asked what

she usually drank and she said she drank mostly tonic
and sometimes beer. I gave her tea with milk and sugar,
and tried to think of something to say. Lovell broke the
ice by asking me if I didn't think her hair was beautiful.
I said that it was very beautiful. Well, it's a lot of work,
she said. I have to wash it twice a week in whites of egg.
Oh there's been plenty of times when I've wanted to
cut it off. People don't understand. People think that if
God crowns you with a beautiful head of hair you ought
to treasure it but it's just as much work as a sinkful of
dishes. You have to wash it and dry it and comb it and
brush it and put it up at night. I know it's hard to understand but honest to God there's days when I would just
like to chop it off but Mummy made me promise on
the Bible that I wouldn't. I'll take it down for you if
you'd like.

I'm telling you the truth, Polly. I am not exaggerat-
ing. She went to the mirror, took a lot of pins out of her
hair, and let it down. There was a great deal of it. I
suppose she could sit on it although I didn't ask. I said
that it was very beautiful several times. Then she said
that she had known I would appreciate it because Lovell
had told her I was artistic and interested in beautiful
things. Well she displayed her hair for some time and
then began the arduous business of getting it back into
place again. It was hard work. Then she went on to
say that some people thought her hair was dyed and
that this made her angry because she felt that women
who dyed their hair were immoral. I asked her if she
would like another cup of tea and she said no. Then I
asked her if she had ever heard Lovell play the piano
and she said no, they didn't have a piano. Then she

looked at Lovell and said that it was time to go. Lovell drove her home and then came back to ask, I suppose, for some words of approval. Of course my heart was broken in two. Here was a great musical career ruined by a head of hair. I told him I never wanted to see her again. He said he was going to marry her and I said I didn't care what he did.

Lovell married Donna-Mae. Uncle Abbott went to the wedding, but Percy kept her word and never saw her daughter-in-law again. Lovell came to the house four times a year to pay a ceremonial call on his mother. He would not go near the piano. He had not only given up his music, he hated music. His simpleminded taste for obsceneness seemed to have transformed itself into simpleminded piety. He had transferred from the Episcopal church to the Hirshmans' Lutheran congregation, which he attended twice on Sundays. They were raising money to build a new church when I last spoke with him. He spoke intimately of the Divinity. "He has helped us in our struggles, again and again. When everything seemed hopeless, He has given us encouragement and strength. I wish I could get you to understand how wonderful He is, what a blessing it is to love Him. . . ." Lovell died before he was thirty, and since everything must have been burned, I don't suppose there was a trace left of his musical career.

But the darkness in the old house seemed, each time we went there, to deepen. Abbott continued his philandering, but when he went fishing in the spring or hunting in the fall Percy was desperately unhappy without him. Less than a year after Lovell's death, Percy was afflicted with some cardiovascular disease. I remember one attack during Sunday dinner. The color drained out of her face, and her breathing became harsh and quick. She excused herself and was mannered enough to say that she had forgotten something. She went into the living room and shut the door, but her accelerated breathing and her groans of pain could be heard. When she returned, there were large splotches of red up the side of her face. "If you don't see a doctor, you will die," Uncle Abbott said.

"You are my husband and you are my doctor," she said.

"I have told you repeatedly that I will not have you as a patient."

"You are my doctor."

"If you don't come to your senses, you will die."

He was right, of course, and she knew it. Now, as she saw the leaves fall, the snow fall, as she said good-bye to friends in railroad stations and vestibules, it was always with a sense that she would not do this again. She died at three in the morning, in the dining room, where she had gone to get a glass of gin, and the family gathered for the last time at her funeral.

There is one more incident. I was taking a plane at Logan Airport. As I was crossing the waiting room, a man who was sweeping the floor stopped me.

"Know you," he said thickly. "I know who you are."

"I don't remember," I said.

"I'm Cousin Beaufort," he said. "I'm your cousin Beaufort."

I reached for my wallet and took out a ten-dollar bill.

"I don't want any money," he said. "I'm your cousin. I'm your cousin Beaufort. I have a job. I don't want any money."

"How are you, Beaufort?" I asked.

"Lovell and Percy are dead," he said. "They buried them in the earth."

"I'm late, Beaufort," I said. "I'll miss my plane. It was nice to see you. Good-bye." And so off to the sea.

Artemis, the Honest Well Digger

Artemis loved the healing sound of rain—the sound of all running water—brooks, gutters, spouts, falls, and taps. In the spring he would drive one hundred miles to hear the cataract at the Wakusha Reservoir. This was not so surprising, since he was a well driller and water was his profession, his livelihood as well as his passion. Water, he thought, was at the root of civilizations. He had seen photographs of a city in Umbria that had been abandoned when the wells went dry. Cathedrals, palaces, farmhouses had all been evacuated by drought—a greater power than pestilence, famine, or war. Men sought water as water sought its level. The pursuit of water accounted for epochal migrations. Man was largely water. Water was man. Water was love. Water was water.

To get the facts out of the way: Artemis drilled with an old Smith & Mathewson chain-concussion rig that struck the planet sixty blows a minute. It made a terrible racket and there had been two complaints. One was from a very nervous house-wife and the other from a homosexual poet who said that the concussion was ruining his meter. Artemis rather liked the noise. He lived with his widowed mother at the edge of town in one of those little conclaves of white houses that are distinguished by their displays of the American flag. You find them on outlying roads—six or seven small houses gathered together for no particular reason. There is no store, no church, nothing central. The lawns on which dogs sleep are well trimmed and everything is neat, but every house flies its Old Glory. This patriotic zeal cannot be traced back to the fact that these people have received an abundance of their country's riches. They haven't. These are hard-working people who lead frugal lives and worry about money. People who have profited splendidly from our economy seem to have no such passion for the Stars and Stripes. Artemis' mother, for example—a hard-working woman—had a flagpole, five little flags stuck into a window box, and a seventh flag hanging from the porch.

His father had chosen his name, thinking that it referred to artesian wells. It wasn't until Artemis was a grown man that he discovered he had been named for the chaste goddess of the hunt. He didn't seem to mind and, anyhow, everybody called him Art. He wore work clothes and in the winter a seaman's knitted cap. His manner with strangers was rustic and shy and something of an affectation, since he read a good deal and had an alert and inquisitive intelligence. His father had learned his trade as an apprentice and had not graduated from high school. He regretted not having an education and was very anxious that his son should go to college. Artemis went to a small college called Laketon in the north of the state and got an engineering degree. He was also exposed to literature through an unusually inspiring professor named Lytle. Physically, there was nothing remarkable about Lytle, but he was the sort of teacher in whose presence students had for many years felt an irresistible desire to read books, write themes, and discuss their most intimate feelings about the history of mankind. Lytle singled out Artemis and encouraged him to read Swift, Donne, and Conrad. He wrote four themes for this course, which Lytle charitably graded A. His ear for prose was damaged by an incurable fascination for words like cacophony, percussion, throbbingly, and thumpingly. This may have had something to do with his profession.

Lytle suggested that he get an editorial job on an engineering journal and he seriously thought about this, but he chose instead to be a well driller. He made his decision one Saturday when he and his father took their rig to the south of the county, where a large house—an estate—had been built. There was a swimming pool and seven baths and the well produced three gallons a minute. Artemis contracted to go down another hundred feet, but even then the take was only six gallons a minute. The enormous, costly, and useless house impressed him with the importance of his trade. Water, water. (What happened in the end was that the owner demolished six upstairs bedrooms to make room for a storage tank, which the local fire department filled twice a week.)

Artemis' knowledge of ecology was confined to water. Going fishing on the first of April, he found the falls of the South Branch foaming with soapsuds. Some of this was bound to leach down to where he worked. Later in the month, he caught a five-pound trout in the stream at Lakeside. This was a phenomenal fish for that part of the world and he stopped to show his catch to the game warden and ask him how it should be cooked. "Don't bother to cook that fish," said the warden. "It's got enough DDT to put you in the hospital. You can't eat these fish anymore. The Government sprayed the banks with DDT about four years ago and the stuff all washed into the brook." Artemis had once dug a well and found DDT, and another had traces of fuel oil. His sense of a declining environment was keen and intensely practical. He contracted to find potable water and if he failed, he lost his shirt. A polluted environment meant for him both sadness at human stupidity and rapaciousness and also a hole in his pocket. He had failed only twice, but the odds were running against him and everybody else.

Another thing: Artemis distrusted dowsers. A few men and two women in the county made their living by divining the presence of subterranean water with forked fruit twigs. The fruit had to have a pit. An apple twig, for example, was no good. When the fruit twig and the diviner's psyche had settled on a site, Artemis would be hired to drill a well. In his experience, the dowsers' average was low and they seldom divined an adequate supply of water, but the fact that some magic was involved seemed to make them irresistible. In the search for water, some people preferred a magician to an engineer. If magic bested knowledge, how simple everything would be: water, water.

Artemis was the sort of man who frequently proposed marriage, but at thirty he still had no wife. He went around for a year or so with the Macklin girl. They were lovers, but when he proposed marriage, she ditched him to marry Jack Bascomb because he was rich. That's what she said. Artemis was melancholy for a month or so, and then he began going around with a divorcée named Maria Petroni who lived on Maple Avenue and was a bank teller. He didn't know, but he had the feeling that Maria was older than he. His ideas about marriage were romantic and a little puerile and he expected his wife to be a fresh-faced virgin. Maria was not. She was a lusty, hard-drinking woman and they spent most of their time together in bed.

One night or early morning, he woke at her side and thought over his life. He was thirty and he still had no bride. He had been dating Maria for nearly two years. Before he moved toward her to wake her, he thought of how humorous, kind, passionate, and yielding she had always been. He thought, while he stroked her backside, that he loved her. Her backside seemed almost too good to be true. The image of a pure, fresh girl like the girl on the oleomargarine package still lingered in some part of his head, but where was she and when would she appear? Was he kidding himself? Was he making a mistake to downgrade Maria for someone he had never seen? When she woke, he asked her to marry him.

"I can't marry you, darling," she said.

"Why not? Do you want a younger man?"

"Yes, darling, but not one. I want seven, one right after the other."

"Oh," he said.

"I must tell you. I've done it. This was before I met you. I asked seven of the best-looking men around to come for dinner. None of them were married. Two of them were divorced. I cooked veal scaloppine. There was a lot to drink and then we all got undressed. It was what I wanted. When they were finished, I didn't feel dirty or depraved or shameful. I didn't feel anything bad at all. Does that disgust you?"

"Not really. You're one of the cleanest people I've ever known. That's the way I think of you."

"You're crazy, darling," she said.

He got up and dressed and kissed her good night, but that was about it. He went on seeing her for a while, but her period of faithfulness seemed to have passed and he guessed that she was seeing other men. He went on looking for a girl as pure and fresh as the girl on the oleomargarine package.

This was in the early fall and he was digging a well for an

old house on Olmstead Road. The first well was running dry. The people were named Filler and they were paying him thirty dollars a foot, which was the rate at that time. He was confident of finding water from what he knew of the lay of the land. When he got the rig going, he settled down in the cab of his truck to read a book. Mrs. Filler came out to the truck and asked if he didn't want a cup of coffee. He refused as politely as he could. She wasn't bad looking at all, but he had decided, early in the game, to keep his hands off the housewives. He wanted to marry the girl on the oleomargarine package. At noon he opened his lunch pail and was halfway through a sandwich when Mrs. Filler came back to the cab. "I've just cooked a nice hamburger for you," she said.

"Oh, no, thank you, ma'am," he said. "I've got three sandwiches here." He actually said ma'am and he sometimes said shucks, although the book he was reading, and reading with interest, was Aldous Huxley.

"You've got to come in now," she said. "I won't take no for an answer." She opened the cab door and he climbed down and followed at her side to the back door.

She had a big butt and a big front and a jolly face and hair that must have been dyed, because it was a mixture of grays and blues. She had set a place for him at the kitchen table and she sat opposite him while he ate his hamburger. She told him directly the story of her life, as was the custom in the United States at that time. She was born in Evansville, Indiana, had graduated from the Evansville North High School, and had been elected apple-blossom queen in her senior year. She then went on to the university in Bloomington, where Mr. Filler, who was older than she, had been a professor. They moved from Bloomington to Syracuse and then to Paris, where he became famous.

"What's he famous for?" asked Artemis.

"You mean you've never heard of my husband?" she said. "J. P. Filler. He's a famous author."

"What did he write?" asked Artemis.

"Well, he wrote a lot of things," she said, "but he's best known for *Shit*."

Artemis laughed, Artemis blushed. "What's the name of the book?" he asked.

"*Shit*," she said. "That's the name of it. I'm surprised you never heard of it. It sold about half a million copies."

"You're kidding," Artemis said.

"No I'm not," she said. "Come with me. I'll show you."

He followed her out of the kitchen through several rooms, much richer and more comfortable than anything he was familiar with. She took from a shelf a book whose title was *Shit*. "My God," said Artemis, "how did he come to write a book like that?"

"Well," she said, "when he was at Syracuse, he got a foundation grant to investigate literary anarchy. He took a year off. That's when we went to Paris. He wanted to write a book about something that concerned everybody, like sex, only by the time he got his grant, everything you could write about sex had been written. Then he got this other idea. After all, it was universal. That's what he said. It concerned everybody. Kings and presidents and sailors at sea. It was just as important as fire, water, earth, and air. Some people might think it was not a very delicate subject to write about, but he hates delicacy, and anyhow, considering the books you can buy these days, *Shit* is practically pure. I'm surprised you never heard about it. It was translated into twelve languages. See." She gestured toward a bookcase, where Artemis read *Merde, Kaka, 糞* and говно. "I can give you a paperback, if you'd like."

"I'd like to read it," said Artemis.

She got a paperback from a closet. "It's too bad he isn't here. He would be glad to autograph it for you, but he's in England. He travels a lot."

"Well, thank you, ma'am," said Artemis. "Thank you for the lunch and the book. I have to get back to work."

He checked the rig, climbed into the cab and put down Huxley for J. P. Filler. He read the book with a certain amount of interest, but his incredulity was stubborn. Except to go to and from college, Artemis had never traveled, and yet he often felt himself to be a traveler, to be among strangers. Walking down a street in China, he would have felt no more alien than he felt at that moment, trying to comprehend the fact that he lived in a world where a man was wealthy and esteemed for having written a book about turds.

That's what it was about: turds. There were all shapes, sizes, and colors, along with a great many descriptions of toilets. Filler had traveled widely. There were the toilets of New Delhi and the toilets of Cairo and he had either imagined or visited the Pope's chambers in the Vatican and the facilities of the Imperial Palace in Tokyo. There were quite a few lyrical descriptions of nature—loose bowels in a lemon grove in Spain, constipation in a mountain pass in Nepal, dysentery on the Greek islands. It was not really a dull book and it had, as she had said, a distinct universality, although Artemis continued to feel that he had strayed into some country like China. He was not a prude, but he used a prudent vocabulary. When a well came too close to a septic tank, he referred to the danger as "fecal matter." He had been "down on" (his vocabulary) Maria many times, but to count these performances and to recall in detail the techniques seemed to diminish the experience. There was, he thought, a height of sexual ecstasy that by its immensity and profoundness seemed to transcend observation. He finished the book a little after five. It looked like rain. He killed the rig, covered it with a tarpaulin, and drove home. Passing a bog, he tossed away his copy of *Shit*. He didn't want to hide it and he would have had trouble describing it to his mother and, anyhow, he didn't want to read it again.

The next day it rained and Artemis got very wet. The rig worked loose and he spent most of the morning making it secure. Mrs. Filler was worried about his health. First she brought him a towel. "You'll catch your death of cold, you darling boy," she said. "Oh, look how curly your hair is." Later, carrying an umbrella, she brought him a cup of tea. She urged him to come into the house and change into dry clothes. He said that he couldn't leave the rig.

"Anyhow," he said, "I never catch cold." As soon as he said this, he began to sneeze. Mrs. Filler insisted that he either come into her house or go home. He was uncomfortable and he gave up around two. Mrs. Filler had been right. By supper-time, his throat was sore. His head was unclear. He took two aspirins and went to bed around nine. He woke after midnight in the hot-and-cold spasms of a high fever. The effect of this was strangely to reduce him to the emotional attitudes of a child. He curled up in an embryonic position, his hands be-tween his knees, alternately sweating and shivering. He felt himself lonely but well protected, irresponsible, and cozy. His father seemed to live again and would bring him, when he came home from work, a new switch for his electric train or a lure for his tackle box. His mother brought him some break-fast and took his temperature. He had a fever of 103 and dozed for most of the morning.

At noon his mother came in to say that there was a lady downstairs to see him. She had brought some soup. He said that he didn't want to see anyone, but his mother seemed doubtful. The lady was a customer. Her intentions were kind. It would be rude to turn her away. He felt too feeble to show any resistance, and a few minutes later Mrs. Filler stood in the doorway with a preserve jar full of broth. "I told him he'd be sick, I told him that yesterday."

"I'll go next door and see if they have any aspirin," said his mother. "We've used ours all up." She left the room and Mrs. Filler closed the door.

"Oh, you poor boy," she said. "You poor boy."

"It's only a cold," he said. "I never get sick."

"But you are sick," she said. "You are sick and I told you you would be sick, you silly boy." Her voice was tremulous and she sat on the edge of his bed and began to stroke his brow. "If you'd only come into my house, you'd be out there today, swinging your sledge hammer." She extended her caresses to his chest and shoulders and then, reaching under the bed-clothes, hit, since Artemis never wore pajamas, pay dirt. "Oh, you lovely boy," said Mrs. Filler. "Do you always get hard this quickly? It's so hard." Artemis groaned and Mrs. Filler went to work. Then he arched his back and let out a muffled yell. The trajectory of his discharge was a little like the fire-balls from a Roman candle and may explain our fascination with these pyrotechnics. Then they heard the front door open and Mrs. Filler left his bed for a chair by the window. Her face was very red and she was breathing heavily.

"All the aspirin they have is baby aspirin," said his mother. "It's pink, but I guess if you take enough of it, it works all right."

"Why don't you go to the drugstore and buy some aspirin?" said Mrs. Filler. "I'll stay with him while you're gone."

"I don't know how to drive," said Artemis' mother. "Isn't that funny? In this day and age. I've never learned how to drive a car." Mrs. Filler was about to suggest that she walk to the drugstore, but she realized that this might expose her position. "I'll telephone the drugstore and see if they deliver," his mother said and left the room with the door open. The telephone was in the hallway and Mrs. Filler remained in her chair. She stayed a few minutes longer and parted on a note of false cheerfulness.

"Now, you get better," she said, "and come back and dig me a nice well."

He was back at work three days later. Mrs. Filler was not there, but she returned around eleven with a load of groceries. At noon, when he was opening his lunch pail, she came out of the house carrying a small tray on which there were two brown, steaming drinks. "I've brought you a toddy," she said. He opened the cab door and she climbed in and sat beside him.

"Is there whiskey in it?" asked Artemis.

"Just a drop," she said. "It's mostly tea and lemon. It will help you get better." Artemis tasted his toddy and thought he had never tasted anything so strong. "Did you read my husband's book?" she asked.

"I looked at it," Artemis said slyly. "I didn't understand it. I mean, I didn't understand why he had to write about that. I don't read very much, but I suppose it's better than some books. The kind of books I really hate are the kind of books where people just walk around and light cigarettes and say things like good morning. They just walk around. When I read a book, I want to read about earthquakes and exploring and tidal waves. I don't want to read about people walking around and opening doors."

"Oh, you silly boy," she said. "You don't know anything."

"I'm thirty years old," said Artemis, "and I know how to drill a well."

"But you don't know what I want," she said.

"You want a well, I guess," he said. "A hundred gallons a minute. Good drinking water."

"I don't mean that. I mean what I want now."

He slumped a little in the seat and unfastened his trousers. She dipped her head, a singular gesture rather like a bird going after seed or water. "Hey, that's great," said Artemis, "that's really great. You want me to tell you when I'm going to come?" She simply shook her head. "Big load's on its way," said Artemis. "Big load's coming down the line. You want me to hold it?" She shook her head. "Ouch," yelled Artemis. "Ouch." One of his limitations as a lover was that, at the most sublime moment, he usually shouted "Ouch, ouch, ouch." Maria had often complained about this. "Ouch," roared Artemis. "Ouch, ouch, ouch," as he was racked by a large orgasm. "Hey, that was great," he said, "that was really great but I'll bet it's unhealthy. I mean, I'll bet if you do that all the time, you'd get to be round-shouldered."

She kissed him tenderly and said, "You're crazy." That made two. He gave her one of his sandwiches.

The rig was then down to three hundred feet. The next day, Artemis hauled up the hammer and lowered the cylinder that measured water. The water was muddy but not soapy and he guessed the take to be about twenty gallons a minute. When Mrs. Filler came out of the house, he told her the news. She didn't seem pleased. Her face was swollen and her eyes were red. "I'll go down another fifteen or twenty feet," Artemis said. "I think you'll have a nice well."

"And then you'll go away," she said, "and never come back." She began to cry.

"Don't cry," said Artemis. "Please don't cry, Mrs. Filler. I hate to see women crying."

"I'm in love," she sobbed loudly.

"Well, I guess a nice woman like you must fall in love pretty often," Artemis said.

"I'm in love with you," she sobbed. "It's never happened to me before. I wake up at five in the morning and start waiting for you to come. Six o'clock, seven o'clock, eight o'clock. It's agony. I can't live without you."

"What about your husband?" asked Artemis cheerfully.

"He knows," she sobbed. "He's in London. I called him last night. I told him. It didn't seem fair to have him come home expecting a loving wife when his wife is in love with someone else."

"What did he say?"

"He didn't say anything. He hung up. He's scheduled to come back tonight. I have to meet the plane at five. I love you, I love you, I love you."

"Well, have to get back to work, ma'am," said Artemis at his most rustic. "You go back to the house now and get some rest." She turned and started for the house. He would have liked to console her—sorrow of any sort distressed him—but he knew that any gesture on his part would be hazardous. He reset the rig and went down another twenty feet, where he estimated the take to be about thirty gallons a minute. At three thirty, Mrs. Filler left. She scowled at him as she drove past. As soon as she had gone, he moved hastily. He capped the well, got his rig onto the truck, and drove home. About nine that night, the phone rang. He thought of not answering or of asking his mother to take it, but his mother was watching television and he had his responsibilities as a well driller. "You've got around thirty-five gallons a minute," he said. "Haversham will install the pump. I don't know whether or not you'll need another storage tank. Ask Haversham. Good-bye."

The next day, he took his shotgun and a package of sandwiches and walked the woods north of the town. He was not much of a wing shot and there weren't many birds, but it pleased him to walk through the woods and pastures and climb the stone walls. When he got home, his mother said, "She was here. That lady. She brought you a present." She passed him a box in which there were three silk shirts and a love letter. Later that evening, when the telephone rang, he asked his mother to say that he was out. It was, of course, Mrs. Filler. Artemis had not taken a vacation in several years and he could see that the time to travel had arrived. In the morning, he went to a travel agency in the village.

The agency was in a dark, narrow room on a dark street, its walls blazing with posters of beaches, cathedrals, and couples in love. The agent was a gray-haired woman. Above her desk was a sign that said, YOU HAVE TO BE CRAZY TO BE A TRAVEL AGENT. She seemed harassed and her voice was cracked with age, whiskey, or tobacco. She chain-smoked. She twice lighted cigarettes when there was a cigarette smoking in the ashtray. Artemis said that he had five hundred to spend and would like to be away for about two weeks. "Well, I suppose you've seen Paris, London, and Disneyland," she said. "Everyone has. There's Tokyo, of course, but they tell me it's a very tiring flight. Seventeen hours in a 707, with a utility stop in Fairbanks. My most satisfied customers these days are the ones who go to Russia. There's a package." She flashed a folder at him. "For three hundred and twenty-eight dollars, you get economy-round-trip air fare to Moscow, twelve days in a first-class hotel with all your meals, free tickets to hockey, ballet, opera, theater, and a pass to the public swimming pool. Side trips to Leningrad and Kiev are optional." He asked what else she might suggest. "Well, there's Ireland," she said, "but it's rainy now. A plane hasn't landed in London for nearly ten days. They stack up at Liverpool and then you take a train down. Rome is cold. So is Paris. It takes three days to get to Egypt. For a two-week trip, the Pacific is out, but you could go to the Caribbean, although reservations are very hard to get. I suppose you'll want to buy souvenirs and there isn't much to buy in Russia."

"I don't want to buy anything," Artemis said. "I just want to travel."

"Take my advice," she said, "and go to Russia."

It seemed the maximum distance that he could place between himself and Mr. and Mrs. Filler. His mother was imperturbable. Most women who owned seven American flags would have protested, but she said nothing but "Go where you want, Sonny. You deserve a change." His visa and passport took a week, and one pleasant evening, he boarded the eight-o'clock Aeroflot from Kennedy to Moscow. Most of the other passengers were Japanese and couldn't speak English and it was a long and a lonely trip.

It was raining in Moscow, so Artemis heard what he liked —the sound of rain. The Japanese spoke Russian and he trailed along behind them across the tarmac to the main building, where they formed a line. The line moved slowly and he had been waiting for an hour or longer when a good-looking young woman approached him and asked, "Are you Mr. Artemis Bucklin? I have very good news for you. Come with me." She found his bag and bucked the lines for customs and immigration. A large black car was waiting for them. "We will go first to your hotel," she said. She had a marked English accent. "Then we will go to the Bolshoi Theater, where our great premier, Nikita Sergeevich Khrushchev, wants to welcome you as a member of the American proletariat. People of many occupations come to visit our beautiful country, but you are the first well driller." Her voice was lilting and she seemed very happy with her news. Artemis was confused, tired, and dirty. Looking out of the car window, he saw an enormous portrait of the premier nailed to a tree. He was frightened.

Why should he be frightened? He had dug wells for rich and powerful people and had met them without fear or shyness. Khrushchev was merely a peasant who, through cunning, vitality, and luck, had made himself the master of a population of over two hundred million. That was the rub; and as the car approached the city, portraits of Khrushchev looked in at Artemis from bakeries, department stores, and lampposts. Khrushchev banners flapped in the wind on a bridge across the Moskva River. In Mayakovsky Square, a large, lighted portrait of Khrushchev beamed down upon his children as they rushed for the subway entrance.

Artemis was taken to a hotel called the Ukraine. "We are already late," the young woman said.

"I can't go anywhere until I've taken a bath and shaved," said Artemis. "I can't go anywhere looking like this. And I would like something to eat."

"You go up and change," she said, "and I'll meet you in the dining room. Do you like chicken?"

Artemis went up to his room and turned on the hot water in his tub. As anyone could guess, nothing happened. He shaved in cold water and was beginning to dress when the hot-water spout made a Vesuvian racket and began to ejaculate rusty and scalding water. He bathed in this, dressed, and went down. She was sitting at a table in the dining room, where his dinner had been served. She had kindly ordered a carafe of vodka, which he drank off before he ate his chicken. "I do not want to hasten you," she said, "but we will be late. I will try to explain. Today is the jubilee of the Battle of Stavitsky. We will go to the

Bolshoi Theater and you will sit on the presidium. I won't be able to sit with you, so you will understand very little of what is said. There will be speeches. Then, after the speeches are over, there will be a reception at the rear of the stage, where our great premier, Nikita Sergeevich Khrushchev, will welcome you as a member of the American proletariat to the Union of Soviet Socialist Republics. I think we should go."

The same car and driver waited for them and, on the trip from the Ukraine to the Bolshoi, Artemis counted seventy portraits of the man he was about to meet. They entered the Bolshoi by a back door. He was taken onto the stage, where the speeches had begun. The jubilee was being televised and the lights for this made the stage as hot as a desert, an illusion that was extended by the fact that the stage was flanked with plastic palm trees. Artemis could understand nothing that was said, but he looked around for the premier. He was not in the principal box. This was occupied by two very old women. At the end of an hour of speeches, his anguish turned to boredom and the unease of a full bladder. At the end of another hour, he was merely sleepy. Then the ceremony ended. There was a buffet backstage and he went there as he had been directed, expecting Khrushchev to make his terrifying appearance, but the premier was not around and when Artemis asked if he was expected, he was given no answer. He ate a sandwich and drank a glass of wine. No one spoke to him. He decided to walk home from the Bolshoi in order to stretch his legs. As soon as he left the theater, a policeman stopped him. He kept repeating the name of his hotel and pointing to his shoes, and when the policeman understood, he gave him directions. Off went Artemis. It seemed to be the same route he had taken in the car, but all the portraits of Khrushchev had vanished. All those pictures that had beamed down on him from bakeries, lampposts, and walls were gone. He thought he was lost, until he crossed a bridge over the Moskva River that he remembered for its banners. They no longer flew. When he reached the hotel, he looked for a large portrait of Khrushchev that had hung in the lobby. Gone. So, like many other travelers before him, he went upstairs to a strange room in a strange country humming the unreality blues. How could he have guessed that Khrushchev had been deposed?

He had breakfast in the dining room with an Englishman who told him the facts. He also suggested that if Artemis needed an interpreter, he should go to the Central Government Agency and not Intourist. He wrote, in the Cyrillic alphabet, an address on a card. He ordered the waiters around officiously in Russian and Artemis was impressed with his fluency; but he was, in fact, one of those travelers who can order fried eggs and hard liquor in seven languages but who can't count to ten in more than one.

There were cabs in front of the hotel and Artemis gave the address to a driver. They took the same route they had taken to the Bolshoi and Artemis was able to recheck the fact that all the portraits of Khrushchev had been removed in two hours or three at the most. It must have taken hundreds of men. The address was a dingy office building with a sign in English as well as Russian. Artemis climbed some shabby stairs to a door that was padded. Why padded? Silence? Madness? He opened the door onto a brightly lighted office and told a striking young woman that he wanted an interpreter to take him around Moscow.

The Russians don't seem to have gotten the bugs out of illumination. There is either too much light or too little and the light the young woman stood in was seedy. She had, however, or so he thought, enough beauty to conquer the situation.

If a thousand portraits of Khrushchev could vanish in three hours, couldn't he fall in love in three minutes? He seemed to. She was about five foot five. He was six feet, which meant that she was the right size, a consideration he had learned to respect. Her brow and the shape of her head were splendid and she stood with her head raised a little, as if she were accustomed to speaking to people taller than herself. She wore a tight sweater that showed her fine breasts and her skirt was also tight. She seemed to be in charge of the office, but in spite of her manifest executive responsibilities, there was not a trace of aggressiveness in her manner. Her femininity was intense. Her essence seemed to lie in two things: a sense of girlishness and the quickness with which she moved her head. She seemed capable of the changeableness, the moodiness of someone much younger. (She was, he discovered later, thirty-two.) She moved her head as if her vision were narrow, as if it moved from object to object, rather than to take in the panorama. Her vision was not narrow, but that was the impression he got. There was some nostalgia in her appearance, some charming feminine sense of the past. "Mrs. Kosiev will take you around," she said. "Without taxi fares, that will be twenty-three rubles." She spoke with exactly the same accent as the woman who had met him at the airport. (He would never know, but they had both learned their English off a tape made at the university in Leningrad by an English governess turned Communist.)

He knew none of the customs of this strange country, but he decided to take a chance. "Will you have dinner with me?" he asked.

She gave him an appraising and pleasant look. "I'm going to a poetry reading," she said.

"Can I come with you?" he asked.

"Why, yes," she said. "Of course. Meet me here at six."

Then she called for Mrs. Kosiev. This was a broad-shouldered woman who gave him a manly handshake but no smile. "Will you please give our guest from the United States the twenty-three-ruble tour of Moscow?" He counted out twenty-three rubles and put them on the desk of the woman with whom he had just fallen in love.

Going down the stairs, Mrs. Kosiev said, "That was Natasha Funaroff. She is the daughter of Marshal Funaroff. They have lived in Siberia. . . ."

After this piece of information, Mrs. Kosiev began to praise the Union of Soviet Socialist Republics and continued this for the rest of the day. They walked a short distance from the office to the Kremlin, where she first took him to the Armory. A long line was waiting at the door, but they bucked this. Inside, they put felt bags over their shoes and Artemis was shown the crown jewels, the royal horse tack, and some of the royal wardrobe. Artemis was bored and had begun to feel terribly tired. They toured three churches in the Kremlin. These seemed to him rich, lofty, and completely mysterious. They then took a cab to the Tretyakov Gallery. Artemis had begun to notice that the smell of Moscow—so far from any tilled land —was the smell of soil, sour curds, sour whey, and earth-stained overalls. It lingered in the massive lobby of the Ukraine. The golden churches of the Kremlin, scoured of their incense, smelled like barns, and in the gallery, the smell of curds and whey was augmented by a mysterious but distinct smell of cow manure. At one, Artemis said he was hungry and they had some lunch. They then went to the Lenin Library and, after that, to a deconsecrated monastery that had been turned into a folk museum. Artemis had seen more than enough, and after the monastery he said that he wanted to return to the hotel. Mrs. Kosiev said that the tour was not completed and that there would be no rebate. He said he didn't care and took a cab back to the Ukraine.

He returned to the office at six. She was waiting in the street, waiting by the door. "Did you have a nice tour?" she asked.

"Oh, yes," said Artemis. "Oh, yes. I don't seem to like museums, but then, I've never been in any and perhaps it's something I could learn."

"I detest museums," she said. She took his arm lightly, lightly touched his shoulder with hers. Her hair was a very light brown—not really blonde—but it shone in the street-lights. It was straight and dressed simply with a short queue in the back, secured with an elastic band. The air was damp and cold and smelled of diesel exhaust. "We are going to hear Luncharvsky," she said. "It isn't far. We can walk."

Oh, Moscow, Moscow, that most anonymous of all anonymous cities! There were some dead flowers on the bust of Chaliapin, but they seemed to be the only flowers in town. Part of the clash of a truly great city on an autumn night is the smell of roasting coffee and (in Rome) wine and new bread and men and women carrying flowers home to a lover, a spouse, or nobody in particular, nobody at all. As it grew darker and the lights went on, Artemis seemed to find none of the excitement of a day's ending. Through a window he saw a child reading a book, a woman frying potatoes. Was it because with all the princes gone and all the palaces still standing one felt, for better or for worse, that a critical spectrum of the city's life had been extinguished? They passed a man carrying three loaves of new bread in a string basket. The man was singing. This made Artemis happy. "I love you, Natasha Funaroff," he said.

"How did you know my name?"

"Mrs. Kosiev told me all about you."

They saw ahead of them the statue of Mayakovsky, although Artemis didn't (doesn't today) know anything about the poet. It was gigantic and tasteless, a relic of the Stalin era that reshaped the whole pantheon of Russian literature to resemble the sons of Lenin. (Even poor Chekhov was given posthumously heroic shoulders and a massive brow.) It grew darker and darker and more lights went on. Then, as they saw the crowd, Artemis saw that the smoke from their cigarettes had formed, thirty or forty feet in the air, a flat, substantial, and unnatural cloud. He supposed this was some process of inversion. Before they reached the square, he could hear Luncharvsky's voice. Russian is a more percussive language than English, less musical but more diverse, and this may account for its carrying power. The voice was powerful, not only in volume but in its emotional force. It seemed melancholy and exalted. Artemis understood nothing beyond the noise. Luncharvsky stood on a platform below the statue of Mayakovsky, declaiming love lyrics to an audience of one thousand or two thousand, who stood under their bizarre cloud or canopy of smoke. He was not singing, but the force of his voice was the force of singing. Natasha made a gesture as if she had brought him to see one of the wonders of the world and he thought that perhaps she had.

He was a traveler, a stranger, and he had traveled this far to see strange things. The dusk was cold, but Luncharvsky was in his shirt sleeves. His shoulders were broad—broad-boned, that is. His arms were long. His hands were large and when he closed them into a fist, as he did every few minutes, the fist seemed massive. He was a tall man. His hair was yellow, not cut and not combed. His eyes had the startling and compelling cast of a man unremittently on the up and up. Artemis

74

had the feeling that not only did he command the attention of the crowd but had anyone there been momentarily inattentive, he would have known it. At the end of the recitation, someone passed him a bouquet of dying chrysanthemums and his suit coat. "I'm hungry," said Artemis.

"We will go to a Georgian restaurant," she said. "A Georgian kitchen is our best kitchen."

They went to a very noisy place where Artemis had chicken for the third time. Leaving the restaurant, she took his arm again, pressed her shoulder against his, and led him down a street. He wondered if she would take him home and if she did, what would he find? Old parents, brothers, sisters, or perhaps a roommate? "Where are we going?" he asked.

"To the park. Is that all right?"

"That's fine," said Artemis. The park, when they reached it, was like any other. There were trees, losing their leaves at that time of year, benches, and concrete walks. There was a concrete statue of a man holding a child on his shoulders. The child held a bird. Artemis supposed they were meant to represent progress or hope. They sat on a bench, he put an arm around her and kissed her. She responded tenderly and expertly and for the next half hour they kissed each other. Artemis felt relaxed, loving, close to sappy. When he stood to straighten the protuberance in his trousers, she took his hand and led him to an apartment house a block or so away. An armed policeman stood by the door. She took what Artemis guessed was an identity card out of her purse. The policeman scrutinized this in a way that was meant to be offensive. He seemed openly bellicose. He sneered, glowered, pointed several times to Artemis, and spoke to her as if she were contemptible. In different circumstances—in a different country—Artemis would have hit him. Finally, they were allowed to pass and they took an elevator—a sort of cage—to another floor. Even the apartment house smelled to Artemis like a farm. She unlocked a door with two keys and led him into a dingy room. There was a bed in one corner. Clothes hung to dry from a string. On a table, there was half a loaf of bread and some scraps of meat. Artemis quickly got out of his clothes, as did she, and they (his choice of words) made love. She cleaned up the mess with a cloth, put a lighted cigarette between his lips, and poured him a glass of vodka. "I don't ever want this to end," Artemis said. "I don't ever want this to end." Lying with her in his arms, he felt a thrilling and galvanic sense of their indivisibility, although they were utter strangers. He was thinking idly about a well he had drilled two years ago and God knows what she was thinking about. "What was it like in Siberia?" he asked.

"Wonderful," she said.

"What was your father like?"

"He liked cucumbers," she said. "He was a marshal until we were sent to Siberia. When we came back, they gave him an office in the Ministry of Defense. It was a little office. There was no chair, no table, no desk, no telephone, nothing. He used to go there in the morning and sit on the floor. Then he died. Now you'll have to go."

"Why?"

"Because it's late and I'll worry about you."

"Can I see you tomorrow?"

"Of course."

"Can you come to my hotel?"

"No, I couldn't do that. It wouldn't be safe for me to be seen in a tourist hotel and, anyhow, I hate them. We can meet in the park. I'll write the address." She left the bed and walked across the room. Her figure was astonishing—it seemed in its perfection to be almost freakish. Her breasts were large, her waist was very slender and her backside was voluminous. She carried it with a little swag, as if it were filled with buckshot. Artemis dressed, kissed her good night and went down. The policeman stopped him but finally let him go, since neither understood anything the other said. When Artemis asked for his key at the hotel, there was some delay. Then a man in uniform appeared, holding Artemis' passport, and extracted the visa.

"You will leave Moscow tomorrow morning," he said. "You will take SAS flight 769 to Copenhagen and change for New York."

"But I want to see your great country," Artemis said. "I want to see Leningrad and Kiev."

"The airport bus leaves at half past nine."

In the morning, Artemis had the Intourist agent in the lobby telephone the interpreters' bureau. When he asked for Natasha Funaroff, he was told there was no such person there; there never had been. Forty-eight hours after his arrival, he was winging his way home. The other passengers on the plane were American tourists and he was able to talk and make friends and pass the time.

Artemis went to work a few days later drilling in hardpan outside the village of Brewster. The site had been chosen by a dowser and he was dubious, but he was wrong. At four hundred feet he hit limestone and a stream of sweet water that came in at one hundred gallons a minute. It was sixteen days after his return from Moscow that he got his first letter from Natasha. His address on the envelope was in English, but there was a lot of Cyrillic writing and the stamps were brilliantly colored. The letter disconcerted his mother and had, she told him, alarmed the postman. To go to Russia was one thing, but to receive letters from that strange and distant country was something else. "My darling," Natasha had written. "I dreamed last night that you and I were a wave on the Black Sea at Yalta. I know you haven't seen that part of my country, but if one were a wave, moving toward shore, one would be able to see the Crimean Mountains covered with snow. In Yalta sometimes when there are roses in bloom, you can see snow falling on the mountains. When I woke from the dream, I felt elevated and relaxed and I definitely had the taste of salt in my mouth. I must sign this letter Fifi, since nothing so irrational could have been written by your loving Natasha."

He answered her letter that night. "Dearest Natasha, I love you. If you will come to this country, I will marry you. I think of you all the time and I would like to show you how we live —the roads and trees and the lights of the cities. It is very different from the way you live. I am serious about all of this, and if you need money for the plane trip, I will send it. If you decided that you didn't want to marry me, you could go home again. Tonight is Halloween. I don't suppose you have that in Russia. It is the night when the dead are supposed to arise, although they don't, of course, but children wander around the streets disguised as ghosts and skeletons and devils and you give them candy and pennies. Please come to my country and marry me."

This much was simple, but to copy her address in the Russian alphabet took him much longer. He went through ten envelopes before he had what he thought was a satisfactory copy. In the morning, before he went to work, he took his letter to the post office. The clerk was a friend. "What in hell are you doing, Art, writing this scribblescrabble to Communists?"

Artemis got rustic. "Well, you see, Sam, I was there for a

day or so and there was this girl." The letter took a twenty-five-cent stamp, a dismal gray engraving of Abraham Lincoln. When Artemis, thinking of the brilliant stamps on her letter, asked if there weren't something livelier, his friend said no.

He got her reply in ten days. "I like to think that our letters cross and I like to think of them flapping their wings at each other somewhere over the Atlantic. I would love to come to your country and marry you or have you marry me here, but we cannot do this until there is peace in the world. I wish we didn't have to depend upon peace for love. I went to the country on Saturday and the birds and the birches and the pines were soothing. I wish you had been with me. A Unitarian doctor of divinity came to the office yesterday looking for an interpreter. He seemed intelligent and I took him around Moscow myself. He told me I didn't have to believe in God to be a Unitarian. God, he told me, is the progress from chaos to order to human responsibility. I always thought God sat on the clouds, surrounded by troops of angels, but perhaps He lives in a submarine, surrounded by divisions of mermaids. Please send me a snapshot and write again. Your letters make me very happy."

"I'm enclosing a snapshot," he wrote. "It's three years old. It was taken at the Wakusha Reservoir. This is the center of the Northeast watershed. I think of you all the time. I woke at three this morning thinking of you. It was a nice feeling. I like the dark. The dark seems to me like a house with many rooms. Sixty or seventy. At night now after work I go skating. I suppose everybody in Russia must know how to skate. I know that Russians play hockey, because they usually beat the Americans in the Olympics. Three to two, seven to two, eight to one. It is beginning to snow. Love, Artemis." He had another struggle with the address.

"Your last letter took eighteen days," she wrote. "I find myself answering your letters before they come, but there's nothing mystical about this, really, for there's an immense clock at the post office with one side black and the other white showing what time it is in different parts of the world. By the time dawn breaks where you are, we are halfway through the day. They have just painted my stairs. The colors are the colors favored by all municipal painters—light brown with a dark-brown border. While they were about it, they splashed a little white paint on the bottom of my mailbox. Now when the lift carries me down, the white paint gives me the illusion that there is a letter from you. I cannot cure myself of this. My heart beats and I run to the box, only to find white paint. Now I ride the lift with my back turned, the drop of paint is so painful."

As he returned from work one night, his mother told him that someone had called from the county seat and said that the call was urgent. Artemis guessed that it must be the Internal Revenue Service. He had had difficulty trying to describe to them the profit and loss in looking for water. He was a conscientious citizen and he called the number. A stranger identified himself as Mr. Cooper and he didn't sound like the Internal Revenue Service. Cooper wanted to see Artemis at once. "Well, you see," Artemis said, "it's my bowling night. Our team is tied for first place and I'd hate to miss the games if we could meet some other time." Cooper was agreeable and Artemis told him where he was working and how to get there. Cooper said he would be there at ten and Artemis went bowling.

In the morning, it began to snow. It looked like a heavy storm. Cooper showed up at ten. He did not get out of his car, but he was so very pleasant that Artemis guessed he was a salesman. Insurance.

"I understand that you've been in Russia."

"Well, I was only there for forty-eight hours. They canceled my visa. I don't know why."

"But you've been corresponding with Russia."

"Yes, there's this girl. I went out with her once. We write each other."

"The State Department is very much interested in your experience. Undersecretary Hurlow would like to talk with you."

"But I didn't really have any experience. I saw some churches and had three chicken dinners and then they sent me home."

"Well, the Undersecretary is interested. He called yesterday and again this morning. Would you mind going to Washington?"

"I'm working."

"It would only take a day. You can take the shuttle in the morning and come back in the afternoon. It won't take long. I think they'll pay your expenses, although this hasn't been decided. I have the information here." He handed the well digger a State Department letterhead that requested the presence of Artemis Bucklin at the new State Department building at nine A.M. on the following day. "If you can make it," Cooper said, "your Government will be very grateful. I wouldn't worry too much about the nine A.M. Nobody much gets to work before ten. It was nice to have met you. If you have any questions, call me at this number." Then he was gone and gone very quickly, because the snow was dense. The well site was in some backwoods where the roads wouldn't be plowed and Artemis drove home before lunch.

Some provincialism—some attachment to the not unpleasant routines of his life—made Artemis feel resistant to the trip to Washington. He didn't want to go, but could he be forced to?

The only force involved was in the phrase that his Government would be grateful. With the exception of the Internal Revenue Service, he had no particular quarrel with his Government and he would have liked—childishly, perhaps—to deserve its gratitude. That night he packed a bag and checked the airline schedules and he was at the new State Department building at nine the next morning.

Cooper had been right about time. Artemis cooled his heels in a waiting room until after ten. He was then taken up two floors, not to see the Undersecretary but to see a man named Serge Belinsky. Belinsky's office was small and bare and his secretary was a peevish southern woman who wore bedroom slippers. Belinsky asked Artemis to fill out some simple bureaucratic forms. When had he arrived in Moscow? when had he left Moscow? where had he stayed? etc. When these were finished, Belinsky had them duplicated and took Artemis up another floor to the office of a man named Moss. Here things were very different. The secretary was pretty and flirtatious and wore shoes. The furniture was not luxurious, but it was a cut above Belinsky's. There were flowers on the desk and a painting on the wall. Artemis repeated the little he remembered, the little there was to remember. When he described the arrangements for his meeting with Khrushchev, Moss laughed; Moss whooped. He was a very elegant young man, so beautifully dressed and polished that Artemis felt himself uncouth, unwashed, and shabby. He was clean enough and mannerly, but his clothes bound at the shoulders and the crotch. "I think the Undersecretary would like to see us now," said Moss, and they went up another flight.

This was an altogether different creation. The floors were carpeted, the walls were paneled, and the secretary wore boots that were buckled with brass and reached up past her skirts, ending God knows where. How far they had come, in such a short distance, from the peevish secretary in bedroom slippers. How Artemis longed for his rig, his work clothes, and his lunch pail. They were served coffee and then the secretary— the one with the boots—dismissed Moss and took him in to the Undersecretary.

Except for a very small desk, there was nothing businesslike about the office. There were colored rugs, sofas, pictures, and flowers. Mr. Hurlow was a very tall man who seemed tired or perhaps unwell. "It was good of you to come, Mr. Bucklin. I'll go straight to the point. I have to go to the Hill at eleven. You know Natasha Funaroff."

"I took her out once. We had dinner and sat in a park."

"You correspond with her."

"Yes."

"Of course, we've monitored your letters. Their government does the same. Our intelligence feels that your letters contain some sort of information. She, as the daughter of a marshal, is close to the government. The rest of her family were shot. She wrote that God might sit in a submarine, surrounded by divisions of mermaids. That same day was the date of our last submarine crisis. I understand that she is an intelligent woman and I can't believe that she would write anything so foolish without its having a second meaning. Earlier she wrote that you and she were a wave on the Black Sea. The date corresponds precisely to the Black Sea maneuvers. You sent her a photograph of yourself beside the Wakusha Reservoir, pointing out that this was the center of the Northeast watershed. This, of course, is not classified information, but it all helps. Later you write that the dark seems to you like a house divided into seventy rooms. This was written ten days before we activated the Seventieth Division. Would you care to explain any of this?"

"There's nothing to explain. I love her."

"That's absurd. You said yourself that you only saw her once. How can you fall in love with a woman you've only seen once? I can't at the moment threaten you, Mr. Bucklin. I can bring you before a committee, but unless you're willing to be more cooperative, this would be a waste of our time. We feel quite sure that you and your friend have worked out a cipher. I can't forbid you to write, of course, but we can stop your letters. What I would like is your patriotic cooperation. Mr. Cooper, whom I believe you've met, will call on you once a week or so and give you the information or rather the misinformation that we would like you to send to Russia, couched, of course, in your cipher, your descriptions of the dark as a house."

"I couldn't do that, Mr. Hurlow. It would be dishonest to you and to Natasha."

The Undersecretary laughed and gave a little girlish tilt to his shoulders. "Well, think it over and call Cooper when you've made up your mind. Of course, the destiny of the nation doesn't depend on your decision. I'm late." He didn't rise, he didn't offer his hand. Artemis, feeling worse than he had felt in Moscow and singing the unreality blues, went past the secretary with the boots and took an elevator down past the secretary with the shoes and the one in bedroom slippers. He got home in time for supper.

He never heard again from the State Department. Had they made a mistake? Were they fools or idle? He would never know. He wrote Natasha four very circumspect letters, omitting his hockey and his bowling scores. There was no reply. He looked for letters from her for a month or so. He thought often of the spot of paint on her mailbox. When it got warmer, there was the healing sound of rain to hear, at least there was that. Water, water.

The Chimera

When I was young and used to go to the circus, there was an act called the Treviso Twins—Maria and Rosita. Rosita used to balance herself on the head of Maria, skulltop to skulltop, and be carried around the ring. Maria, as a result of this strenuous exercise, had developed short, muscular legs and a comical walk, and whenever I see my wife walking away from me I remember Maria Treviso. My wife is a big woman. She is one of the five daughters of Colonel Boysen, a Georgia politician, who was a friend of Calvin Coolidge. He went to the White House seven times, and my wife has a heart-shaped pillow embroidered with the word "LOVE" that was either the work of Mrs. Coolidge or was at one time in her possession. My wife and I are terribly unhappy together, but we have three beautiful children, and we try to keep things going. I do what I have to do, like everyone else, and one of the things I have to do is to serve my wife breakfast in bed. I try to fix her a nice breakfast, because this sometimes improves her disposition, which is generally terrible. One morning not long ago, when I brought her a tray she clapped her hands to her face and began to cry. I looked at the tray to see if there was anything wrong. It was a nice breakfast—two hard-boiled eggs, a piece of Danish, and a Coca-Cola spiked with gin. That's what she likes. I've never learned to cook bacon. The eggs looked all right and the dishes were clean, so I asked her what was the matter. She lifted her hands from her eyes—her face was wet with tears and her eyes were haggard—and said, in the Boysen-family accent, "I cannot any longer endure being served breakfast in bed by a hairy man in his underwear."

I took a shower and dressed and went to work, but when I came home that night I could see that things were no better; she was still offended by my appearance that morning.

I cook most of the dinners on a charcoal grill in the back yard. Zena doesn't like to cook and neither do I, but it's pleasant being out of doors, and I like tending the fire. Our neighbors, Mr. Livermore and Mr. Kovacs, also do a lot of cooking outside. Mr. Livermore wears a chef's hat and an apron that says "Name Your Pizen," and he also has a sign that says DANGER. MEN COOKING. Mr. Kovacs and I don't wear costumes, but I think we're more serious-minded. Mr. Kovacs once cooked a leg of lamb and another time a little turkey. We had hamburger that night, and I noticed that Zena didn't seem to have any appetite. The children ate heartily, but as soon as they were through—perhaps they sensed a quarrel—slipped off into the television room to watch the quarrels there. They were right about the quarrel. Zena began it.

"You're so inconsiderate," she thundered. "You never think of me."

"I'm sorry, darling," I said. "Wasn't the hamburger done?" She was drinking straight gin, and I didn't want a quarrel.

"It wasn't the hamburger—I'm used to the garbage you cook. What I have for dinner is no longer of any importance to me. I've learned to get along with what I'm served. It's just that your whole attitude is so inconsiderate."

"What have I done, darling?" I always call her darling, hoping that she may come around.

"What have you done? What have you done?" Her voice rose, and her face got red, and she got to her feet and, standing above me, she screamed, "You've ruined my life, that's what you've done."

"I don't see how I've ruined your life," I said. "I guess you're disappointed—lots of people are—but I don't think it's fair to blame it all on your marriage. There are lots of things I wanted to do—I wanted to climb the Matterhorn—but I wouldn't blame the fact that I haven't on anyone else."

"You. Climb the Matterhorn. Ha. You couldn't even climb the Washington Monument. At least I've done that. I had important ambitions. I might have been a businesswoman, a TV writer, a politician, an actress. I might have been a congresswoman!"

"I didn't know you wanted to be a congresswoman," I said.

"That's the trouble with you. You never think of me. You never think of what I might have done. You've ruined my life!" Then she went upstairs to her bedroom and locked the door.

Her disappointment was painfully real, I knew, although I thought I had given her everything I had promised. The false promises, the ones whose unfulfillment made her so miserable, must have been made by Colonel Boysen, but he was dead. None of her sisters was happily married, and how disastrously unhappy they had been had never struck me until that night. I mean, I had never put it together. Lila, the oldest, had lost her husband while they were taking a stroll on a high cliff above the Hudson. The police had questioned her, and the whole family, including me, had been indignant about their suspiciousness, but mightn't she have given him a little push? Stella, the next oldest, had married an alcoholic, who systematically drank himself out of the picture. But Stella had been capricious and unfaithful, and mightn't her conduct have hastened his death? Jessica's husband had been drowned mysteriously in Lake George when they had stopped at a motel and gone for a night swim. And Laura's husband had been killed in a freak automobile accident while Laura was at the wheel. Were they murderesses, I wondered—had I married into a family of incorrigible murderesses? Was Zena's disappointment at not being a congresswoman powerful enough to bring her to plot my death? I didn't think so. I seemed much less afraid for my life than to need tenderness, love, loving, good cheer—all the splendid and decent things I knew to be possible in the world.

The next day at lunch, a man from the office told me that he had met a girl named Lyle Smythe at a party and that she was a tart. This was not exactly what I wanted, but my need to reacquaint myself with the tenderer members of the sex was excruciating. We said good-bye in front of the restaurant, and then I went back in to look up Lyle Smythe's number in the telephone book and see if I could make a date. One of the light bulbs in the lamp that illuminated the directory was dead and the print seemed faint and blurred to me. I found her name, but it was on the darkest part of the page, where the binding and the clasp drew the book together, and I had trouble reading the number. Was I losing my sight? Did I need glasses or was it only because the light was dim? Was there some irony in the idea of a man who could no longer read a telephone book trying to find a mistress? By moving my head up and down like a duck I found that I could read the exchange, and I struck a match to read the number. The lighted match fell out of my fingers and set fire to the page. I blew on the fire to extinguish it, but this only raised the flames, and I had to beat out the fire with my hands. My first instinct was to turn my head around to see if I had been watched, and I had been, by a tall, thin man wearing a plastic hat cover and a blue transparent raincoat. His figure startled me. He seemed to represent something—conscience, or evil—and I went back to the office and never made the call.

That night, when I was washing the dishes, I heard Zena speak to me from the kitchen door. I turned and saw her standing there, holding my straight razor. (I have a heavy beard and shave with a straight-edged razor.) "You'd better not leave things like this lying around," she shouted. "If you know what's good for you, you'd better not leave things like this lying around. There are plenty of women in the world who would cut you to ribbons for what I've endured . . ." I wasn't afraid. What *did* I feel? I don't know. Bewilderment, crushing bewilderment, and some strange tenderness for poor Zena.

She went upstairs, and I went on washing the dishes and wondering if scenes like this were common on the street where I live. But God, oh, God, how much then I wanted some kind of loveliness, softness, gentleness, humor, sweetness, and kindness. And when the dishes were done, I went out of the house, out of the back door. In the dusk Mr. Livermore was dyeing the brown spots on his lawn with a squirt gun. Mr. Kovacs was cooking two rock hens. I did not invent this world, with all its paradoxes, but it was never my good fortune to travel, and since yards like these are perhaps the most I will see of life, I looked at the scene—even the DANGER. MEN COOKING sign— with intentness and feeling. There was music in the air—there always is—and it heightened my desire to see a beautiful woman. Then a sudden wind sprang up, a rain wind, and the smell of a deep forest—although there are no forests in my part of the world—mushroomed among the yards. The smell excited me, and I remembered what it was like to feel young and happy, wearing a sweater and clean cotton pants, and walking through the cool halls of the house where I was raised and where, in the summer, the leaves hung beyond all the open doors and windows in a thick curtain of green and gold. I didn't remember my youth—I seemed to recapture it. Even more—because, given some self-consciousness by retrospect, I esteemed as well as possessed the bold privileges of being young. There was the music of a waltz from the Livermores' television set. It must have been a commercial for deodorants, girdles, or ladies' razors, the air was so graceful and so somber. Then, as the music faded—the forest smell was still sharp in the air—I saw her walk up the grass, and she stepped into my arms.

Her name was Olga. I can't change her name any more than I can change her other attributes. She was nothing, I know, but an idle reverie. I've never fooled myself about this. I've imagined that I've won the daily double, climbed the Matterhorn, and sailed, first class, for Europe, and I suppose I imagined Olga out of the same need for escape or tenderness, but, unlike any other reverie I've ever known, she came with a dossier of facts. She was beautiful, of course. Who, under the circumstances, would invent a shrew, a harridan? Her hair was dark, fragrant, and straight. Her face was oval, her skin was olive-colored, although I could hardly make out her features in the dusk. She had just come from California on the train. She had come not to help me but to ask my help. She needed protection from her husband, who was threatening to follow her. She needed love, strength, and counsel. I held her in my arms, basking in the grace and warmth of her presence. She cried when she spoke of her husband, and I knew what he looked like. I can see him now. He was an army sergeant. There were scars on his thick neck, left from an attack of boils. His face was red. His hair was yellow. He wore a double row of campaign ribbons on a skintight uniform. His breath smelled of rye and toothpaste. I was so delighted by her company, her dependence, that I wondered— not at all seriously—if I wasn't missing a stitch. Did Mr. Livermore, dyeing his grass, have a friend as beautiful as mine? Did Mr. Kovacs? Did we share our disappointments this intimately? Was there such hidden balance and clemency in the universe that our needs were always requited? Then it began to rain. It was time for her to go, but we took such a long, sweet hour to say good-bye that when I went back into the kitchen I was wet through to the skin.

On Wednesday night I always take my wife to the Chinese restaurant in the village, and then we go to the movies. We order the family dinner for two, but my wife eats most of it. She's a big eater. She reaches right across the table and grabs my egg roll, empties the roast duck onto her plate, takes my fortune cookie away from me, and then when she's done she sighs a deep sigh and says, "Well, you certainly stuffed yourself." On Wednesdays I always eat a big lunch in town, so I won't be hungry. I always have the calf's liver and bacon or something like that, to fill me up.

As soon as I stepped into the restaurant that night, I thought I would see Olga. I hadn't known that she would return—I hadn't thought about it—but since I've seen the summit of the Matterhorn in my dreams much more than once, mightn't she reappear? I felt happy and expectant. I was glad that I had on my new suit and had remembered to get a haircut. I wanted her to see me at my best, and I wanted to see her in a brighter light than she had appeared in that rainy night. Then I noticed that the Muzak was playing the same somber and graceful waltz that I had heard coming from the Livermores' television, and I thought that perhaps this was no more than a deception of the music—some simple turn of memory that had fooled me as I had been fooled by the smell of the rain into thinking that I was young.

There was no Olga. I had no consolation. Then I felt desperate, desolate, crushed. I noticed how Zena smacked her lips and gave me a challenging glare, as if she was daring me to touch the shrimp foo-yong. But I wanted Olga, and the force of my need seemed to reestablish her reality. How could anything I desired so ardently be unreal? The music was only a coincidence. I straightened up again and looked around the place cheerfully, expecting her to come in at any minute, but she never did.

I didn't think she would be at the movies—I knew she didn't like movies—but I still had the feeling that I would see her that night. I didn't deceive myself—I want to make this clear; I knew she was unreal, and yet she seemed to have some punctuality, some order, some schedule of engagements, and above all I needed her. After my wife went to bed I sat on the edge of the bathtub reading the newspaper. My wife doesn't like me to sit in the kitchen or the living room, so I read in the bathroom, where the light is bright. I was reading when Olga came in. There was no waltz music, no rain, nothing that could account for her presence, excepting my loneliness. "Oh my darling," I said, "I thought you were going to meet me at the restaurant." She said something about not wanting to be seen by my wife. Then she sat down beside me on the bathtub, I put my arms around her, and we talked about her plans. She was looking for an apartment. She was then living in a cheap hotel, and she was having trouble finding a job. "It's too bad you can't type and take shorthand," I remember telling her. "It might almost be worthwhile going to school. . . . I'll look around and see if I can find anything. Sometimes there's an opening for a receptionist. . . . You could do that, couldn't you? I won't let you be a hat-check girl or a restaurant hostess. No, I won't let you. I'd rather pay your salary until something better comes along. . . ."

My wife threw open the bathroom door. Women's hair curlers, like grass dye and funny signs, only seem to me reminders of the fact that we must find more serious and finer things upon which to comment, and I will only say that my wife wears so many and such bellicose hair curlers that anybody trying to romance her would lose an eye. "You're talking to yourself," she thundered. "You can be heard all over the neighborhood. They'll think you're nuts. And you woke me up. You woke me out of a sound sleep, and you know that if my first sleep is interrupted I can't ever get to sleep again." She went to the medicine cabinet and took a sleeping pill. "If you want to talk to yourself," she said, "go on up to the attic." She went into her bedroom and locked the door.

A few nights later, when I was cooking some hamburgers in the back yard, I saw what looked to be some rain clouds rising in the south. I thought this was a good sign. I wanted some news of Olga. After I had washed the dishes I went out onto the back porch and waited. It isn't really a porch—just a little wooden platform with four steps above the garbage pail. Mr. Livermore was on his porch, and Mr. Kovacs was on his, and I wondered were they waiting as I was for a chimera. If I went over, for instance, and asked Mr. Livermore if his was blonde or dark-haired, would he understand? For a minute I wanted terribly to confide in someone. Then the waltz began to play, and just as the music faded she ran up the steps.

Oh, she was very happy that night! She had a job. I knew all about this, because I'd found the job for her. She was working as a receptionist in the same building where I worked. What I didn't know was that she had found an apartment—not a real apartment but a furnished room with a kitchen and bath of her own. This was just as well, because all her furniture was in California. Would I come and see the apartment? Would I come now? We could take a late train in and spend the night there. I said that I would, but first I had to go into the house and see that the children were all right. I went upstairs to the children's room. They were asleep. Zena had already locked herself in. I went into the bathroom to wash my hands and found on the basin a note, written by Betty-Ann, my oldest daughter. "Dere Daddy," she had written, "do not leave us."

This convergence of reality and unreality was meaningless. The children wouldn't know anything about my delusion. The back porch, to their clear eyes, would seem empty. The note would only reflect their inescapable knowledge of my unhappiness. But Olga was waiting on the back porch. I seemed to feel her impatience, to see the way she swung her long legs, glanced at her wristwatch (a graduation present), and smoked a cigarette, and yet I also seemed nailed to the house by the children's plea. I could not move. I remembered a parade in the village I had taken my youngest son to not long ago. It was the annual march of some provincial and fraternal order. There were two costumed bands and half a dozen platoons of the fraternity. The marchers, the brotherhood, seemed mostly to be marginal workmen—post-office clerks and barbers, I guess. The weather couldn't have accounted for my attitude, because I remembered clearly that it was fair and cool, but the effect of the parade upon me was as somber as if I had stood on some gallows hill. In the ranks I saw faces lined by drink, harried by hard work, wasted by worry, and stamped invariably with disappointment, as if the gala procession was meant to prove that life is a force of crushing compromise. The music was boisterous, but the faces and the bodies were the faces and bodies of compromised men, and I remembered getting to my feet and staring into the last of the ranks, looking for someone with clear features that would dispel my sober feelings. There was no one. Sitting in the bathroom, I seemed to join the marchers. I seemed to experience for the first time in my life what they must all have known—racked and torn with the desire to escape and nailed through the heart by a plea. I ran downstairs, but she had gone. No pretty woman waits very long for anyone. She was a fiction, and yet I couldn't bring her back, any more than I could change the fact that her wristwatch was a graduation present and that her name was Olga.

She didn't come back for a week, although Zena was in terrible shape and there seemed to be some ratio, some connection, between her obstreperousness and my ability to produce a phantom. Every night at eight, the Livermores' television played the somber and graceful waltz, and I was out there every night. Ten days passed before she returned. Mr. Kovacs was cooking. Mr. Livermore was dyeing his grass.

The music had just begun to fade when she appeared. Something had changed. She held her head down. What was wrong? As she came up the steps, I saw that she had been drinking. She was drunk. She began to cry as soon as I took her in my arms. I stroked her soft, dark hair, perfectly happy to support and hold her, whatever had happened. She told me everything. She had gone out with a man from the office. He had got her drunk and seduced her. She had felt too ashamed of herself to go to work in the morning, and had spent some time in a bar. Then, half drunk, she had gone to the office to confront her seducer, and there had been a disorderly scene, during which she was fired. It was I she had betrayed, she told me. She didn't care about herself. I had given her a chance to lead a new life and she had failed me. I caught myself smiling fatuously at the depth of her dependence, the ardor with which she clung to me. I told her that it would be all right, that I would find her another job and pay her rent in the meantime. I forgave her, and she promised to return the next evening.

I rushed outdoors the next night—I was there long before eight o'clock, but she didn't come. She wasn't thoughtless. I knew that. She wouldn't deliberately disappoint me. She must be in trouble again, but how could I help her? How could I get word to her? I seemed to know the place where she lived. I knew its smells, its lights, the van Gogh reproduction, and the cigarette burns on the end table, but even so, the room didn't exist, and I couldn't look there. I thought of looking for her in the neighborhood bars, but I was not yet this insane. I waited for her again on the following night. I was worried but not angry when she didn't come, since she was, after all, such a defenseless child. The next night, it rained, and I knew she couldn't come, because she didn't have a raincoat. She had told me that. The next day was Saturday, and I thought she might put off her return until Monday, the weekend train and bus schedules being so erratic. This seemed sensible to me, but I was so convinced that she would return on Monday that when she failed me I felt terribly disappointed and lost. She came back on Thursday. It was the same hour of day; I heard the same graceful waltz. Even down the length of the yard, long before she reached the porch, I could see she was staggering. Her hair was disheveled, her dress was torn, her wristwatch missing. I asked her, for some reason, about the wristwatch, but she couldn't remember where it was. I took her in my arms, and she told me what had happened. Her seducer had returned. She had let him in; she had let him move in. He stayed three days, and then they gave a party for some friends of his. The party was late and noisy, and the landlady called the police, who raided the place and took Olga off to jail, where she was charged with using the room for immoral purposes, She was in the Women's House of Detention for three days before her case was heard. A kindly judge gave her a suspended sentence. Now she was going back to California, back to her husband. She was no better than he, she kept insisting; they were two of a kind. He had wired her the money, and she was taking the night train. I tried to persuade her to stay and begin a new life. I was willing to go on helping her; I would take her on any terms. I shook her by the shoulders—I remember that. I remember shouting at her, "You can't go! You can't go! You're all I have. If you go, it will only prove that even the most transparent inventions of my imagination are subject to lust and age. You can't go! You can't leave me alone!"

"Stop talking to yourself," my wife shouted from the television room, and at that moment a thought occurred to me: Since I had invented Olga, couldn't I invent others—dark-eyed blondes, vivacious redheads with marbly skin, melancholy brunettes, dancers, women who sang, lonely housewives? Tall women, short women, sad women, women whose burnished hair flowed to their waists, sloe-eyed, squint-eyed, violet-eyed beauties of all kinds and ages could be mine. Mightn't Olga's going only mean that she was making room for someone else?

*Mene, Mene, Tekel,
Upharsin*

Coming back from Europe that year, I was booked on an old DC-7 that burned out an engine in mid-Atlantic. Most of the passengers seemed either asleep or drugged, and in the forward section of the plane no one saw the flames but a little girl, an old man, and me. When the fire died down, the plane veered violently, throwing open the door to the crew's quarters. There I saw the crew and the two stewardesses, wearing inflated life jackets. One of the stewardesses shut the door, but the captain came out a few minutes later and explained, in a fatherly whisper, that we had lost an engine and were heading either for Iceland or Shannon. Some time later, he came in and said we would be landing in London in half an hour. Two hours later, we landed at Orly, to the astonishment of all those who had been asleep. We boarded another DC-7 and started back across the Atlantic, and when we finally landed at Idlewild we had been traveling in cramped conditions for about twenty-seven hours.

I took a bus into New York and a cab to Grand Central Station. It was an off hour—seven thirty or eight o'clock in the evening. The newsstands were shut, and the few people on the streets were alone and seemed lonely. There was not a train to where I was going for an hour, so I went into a restaurant near the station and ordered the *plat du jour*. The dilemma of an expatriated American eating his first restaurant meal at home has been worked over too often to be repeated here. After paying the check, I went down some stairs to find the amenities. The place I entered had marble partitions—a gesture, I suppose, toward ennobling this realm. The marble was a light brown—it might have been a *giallo antico*, but then I noticed Paleozoic fossils beneath the high polish and guessed that the stone was a madrepore. The near side of the polish was covered with writing. The penmanship was legible, although it had no character or symmetry. What was unusual was the copiousness of the writing and the fact that it was organized into panels, like the pages of a book. I had never seen anything like this before. My deepest instinct was to overlook the writing and study the fossils, but isn't the writing of a man more lasting and wonderful than a Paleozoic coral? I read:

It had been a day of triumph in Capua. Lentulus, returning with victorious eagles, had amused the populace with the sports of the amphitheater to an extent hitherto unknown, even in that luxurious city. The shouts of revelry died away; the roar of the lion had ceased; the last loiterer retired from the banquet, and the lights in the palace of the victor were extinguished. The moon, piercing the tissue of

fleecy clouds, silvered the dewdrop on the corselet of the
Roman sentinel and tipped the dark waters of Vulturnus
with wavy, tremulous light. It was a night of holy calm,
when the zephyr sways the young spring leaves and whis-
pers among the hollow reeds its dreamy music. No sound
was heard but the last sob of some weary wave, telling its
story to the smooth pebbles of the beach, and then all was
still as the breast when the spirit has parted. . . .

I read no more, although there was more to read. I was
tired and in some way disarmed by the fact that I had not
been home for years. The chain of circumstances that could
impel a man to copy this gibberish on marble was unimagin-
able. Was this a sign of some change in the social climate,
the result of some new force of repression? Or was it simply
an indication of the fact that man's love of florid prose is
irresistible? The sonorities of the writing had the tenacity of
bad music, and it was difficult to forget them. Had some profound change in the psyche of my people taken place during
my absence? Was there some breakdown in the normal lines
of communication, some inordinate love of the romantic past?

I spent the next week or ten days traveling in the
Middle West. I was waiting one afternoon in the Union
Station in Indianapolis for a New York train. The train was
late. The station there—proportioned like a cathedral and
lit by a rose window—is a gloomy and brilliant example of
that genre of architecture that means to express the mystery
and drama of travel and separation. The colors of the rose
window, limpid as a kaleidoscope, dyed the marble walls and
the waiting passsengers. A woman with a shopping bag stood

in a panel of lavender. An old man slept in a pool of yellow light. Then I saw a sign directing the way to the men's room, and I wondered if I might not find there another example of that curious literature I had discovered in the first hours of my return. I went down some stairs into a cavernous basement, where a shoeshine man slept in a chair. The walls again were marble. This was a common limestone—a silicate of calcium and magnesium, grained with some metalliferous gray ore. My hunch had been right. The stone was covered with writing, and it had, at a glance, a striking fitness, since it served as a reminder of the fact that it was on walls that the earliest writings and prophecies of man appeared. The penmanship was clear and symmetrical, the work of someone gifted with an orderly mind and a steady hand. Please try to imagine the baneful light, the stale air, and the sounds of running water in that place as I read:

The great manor house of Wallowyck stood on a hill above the smoky mill town of X——burgh, its countless mullioned windows seeming to peer censoriously into the dark and narrow alleys of the slums that reached from the park gates to the smoking mills on the banks of the river. It was in the fringes of this wooded park that, unknown to Mr. Wallow, I spent the most lighthearted hours of my youth, roaming there with a slingshot and a sack for transporting my geological specimens. The hill and its forbidding ornament stood between the school I attended and the hovel where I lived with my ailing mother and my drunken father. All my friends took the common path around the hill, and it was only I who climbed the walls of Wallow Park and spent my afternoons in this forbidden demesne.

The lawns, the great trees, the sound of fountains, and the solemn atmosphere of a dynasty are dear to me to this

day. The Wallows had no arms, of course, but the sculptors they employed had improvised hundreds of escutch-
eons and crests that seemed baronial at a distance but that,
on examination, petered out modestly into geometrical
forms. Their chimneys, gates, towers, and garden benches
were thus crested. Another task of the sculptors had been
to make representations of Mr. Wallow's only daughter,
Emily. There was Emily in bronze, Emily in marble, Emily
as the Four Seasons, the Four Winds, the Four Times of
Day, and the Four Principal Virtues. In a sense, Emily was
my only companion. I walked there in the autumn, watching the wealth of color fall from the trees to the lawns. I
walked there in the bitter snow. I watched there for the first
signs of spring, and smelled the fine perfume of wood
smoke from the many crested chimneys of the great house
above me. It was while wandering there on a spring day
that I heard a girlish voice crying for help. I followed the
voice to the banks of a little stream, where I saw Emily.
Her lovely feet were naked, and stuck to one, like some
manacle of evil, was the writhing form of a viper.

I plucked the viper from her foot, lanced the wound
with my pocketknife, and sucked the poison from her
bloodstream. Then I took off my humble shirt, stitched
together for me by my dear mother from some discarded
blueprint linen that she had found, during her daily forag-
ing, in an architect's ashcan. When the wound was cleansed
and bound, I gathered Emily in my arms and ran up the
lawn towards the great doors of Wallowyck, which rumbled open at my ring. A butler stood there, pallid at the
sight.

"What have you done to our Emily?" he cried.

"He has done nothing but save my life," said Emily.

Then from the dusk of the hall emerged the bearded
and ruthless Mr. Wallow. "Thank you for saving the life

of my daughter," he said gruffly. Then he looked at me more closely, and I saw tears rise in his eyes. "Someday you will be rewarded," he said. "That day will come."

The ruin of my linen shirt obliged me to tell my parents that evening about my adventure. My father was drunk, as usual. "You will receive no reward from that beast!" he roared. "Neither in this world nor in Heaven nor in Hell!"

"Please, Ernest," my mother sighed, and I went to her and held her hands, dry with fever.

Drunk as he was, it seemed that my father possessed the truth, for, in the years that followed, no sign of gratitude, no courtesy, no trifling remembrance, no hint of indebtedness came to me from the great house on the hill.

In the stern winter of 19—, the mills were shut down by Mr. Wallow, in a retaliative gesture at my struggle to organize a labor union. The stillness of the mills—those smokeless chimneys—was a blow at the heart of X——burgh. My mother lay dying. My father sat in the kitchen drinking Sterno. Sickness, hunger, cold, and disease dominated every hovel. The snow in the streets, unbesmirched by the mill smoke, had an accusatory whiteness. It was on the day before Christmas that I led the union delegation, many of them scarcely able to walk, up to the great doors of Wallowyck and rang. It was Emily who stood there when the doors were opened. "You!" she cried. "You who saved my life, why are you killing my father?" Then the doors rumbled shut.

I managed that evening to gather a little grain, and made some porridge of this for my mother. I was spooning this into her thin lips when our door opened and in stepped Jeffrey Ashmead, Mr. Wallow's advocate.

"If you have come," I said, "to persecute me for my demonstration at Wallowyck this afternoon, you have come in vain. There is no pain on earth greater than that which I suffer now, as I watch my mother die."

"I have come about other business," he said. "Mr. Wallow is dead."

"Long live Mr. Wallow!" shouted my father from the kitchen.

"Please come with me," said Mr. Ashmead.

"What business can I have with you, sir?"

"You are the heir to Wallowyck—its mines, its mills, its moneys."

"I do not understand."

There was a piercing sob from my mother. She seized my hands in hers and said, "The truth of the past is no harsher than the truth of our sad lives! I have wanted to shelter you all these years from the truth but you are his only son. As a girl, I waited on table at the great house, and was taken advantage of on a summer's night. It has contributed to your father's destruction."

"I will go with you, sir," I said to Mr. Ashmead. "Miss Emily knows of this?"

"Miss Emily," he said, "has fled."

I returned that evening, and entered the great doors of Wallowyck as its master. But there was no Miss Emily. Before the New Year had come, I had buried both of my parents, reopened the mills on a profit-sharing basis, and brought prosperity to X——burgh, but I, living alone in Wallowyck, knew a loneliness that I had never tasted before. . . .

I was appalled, of course. I felt sick. The matter-of-factness of my surroundings made the puerility of this tale nauseating. I hurried back to the noble waiting room, with its limpid panels of colored light, and sat down near a rack of paperback books. Their lurid covers and their promise of graphic descriptions of sexual commerce seemed to tie in with what I had just read. What had happened, I supposed, was that, as pornography moved into the public domain, those marble walls, those im-memorial repositories of such sport, had been forced, in self-defense, to take up the more refined task of literature. I found the idea revolutionary and disconcerting, and wondered if in a year or two I would be able to read the poetry of Sara Teas-dale in a public toilet, while the King of Sweden honored some dirty-minded brute. Then my train came in, and I was happy to get out of Indianapolis and leave, as I hoped, my discovery with the Middle West.

I went up to the club car and had a drink. We belted east-ward over Indiana, scaring the cows and the chickens, the horses and the pigs. People waved at the train as it passed —a little girl holding a doll upside down, an old man in a wheelchair, a woman standing in a kitchen doorway with her hair in pin curls, a young man sitting on a freight truck. You could feel the train leap forward in the straighta-way, the whistle blew, the warning bells at the grade cros-sings went off like a coronary thrombosis, and the track joints beat out a jazz bass, versatile, exhilarating, and fleet, like some brilliant improvisation on the beating of a heart, and the wind in the brake boxes sounded like the last, hoarse recordings poor Billy Holiday ever made. I had two more drinks. When I opened the door of the lavatory in the next sleeping car and saw that the walls were cov-ered with writing, it seemed to me like a piece of very bad news.

I didn't want to read any more—not then. Wallowyck had been enough for one day. I wanted only to go back to the club car and have another drink and assert my healthy indifference to the fancies of strangers. But the writing was there, and it was irresistible—it seemed to be some part of my destiny—and, although I read it with bitter unwillingness, I read through

the first paragraph. The penmanship was the most command-
ing of all.

> Why does not everyone who can afford it have a gera-
> nium in his window? It is very cheap. Its cheapness is next
> to nothing if you raise it from seed or from a slip. It is a
> beauty and a companion. It sweetens the air, rejoices the
> eye, links you with nature and innocence, and is something
> to love. And if it cannot love you in return, it cannot hate
> you, it cannot utter a hateful thing even for your neglect-
> ing it, for though it is all beauty, it has no vanity, and such
> being the case, and living as it does purely to do you good
> and afford pleasure, how will you be able to neglect it?
> But, pray, if you choose a geranium . . .

Back in the club car, it was getting dark. I was disturbed by
these tender sentiments and depressed by the general gloom of
the countryside at that time of day. Was what I had read the
expression of some irrepressible love of quaintness and innocence? Whatever it was, I felt then a manifest responsibility to
declare what I had discovered. Our knowledge of ourselves
and of one another, in a historical moment of mercurial change,
is groping. To hedge our observation, curiosity, and reflection
with indifference would be sheer recklessness. My three chance
encounters proved that this kind of literature was widespread.
If these fancies were recorded and diagnosed, they might
throw a brilliant illumination onto our psyche and bring us
closer to the secret world of the truth. My search had its un-
conventional aspects, but if we are any less than shrewd,
courageous, and honest with ourselves we are contemptible. I
had six friends who worked for foundations, and I decided to
call their attention to the phenomenon of the writing in public

toilets. I knew they had financed poetry, research in zoology, studies of the history of stained glass and of the social significance of high heels, and, at that moment, the writing in public toilets appeared to be an avenue of truth that demanded exploration.

When I got back to New York, I arranged a lunch for my friends, in a restaurant in the Sixties that has a private dining room. At the end of the meal, I made my speech. My best friend there was the first to answer. "You've been away too long," he said. "You're out of touch. We don't go for that kind of thing over here. I can only speak for myself, of course, but I think the idea is repulsive." I glanced down and saw that I was wearing a brocade double-breasted vest and pointed yellow shoes, and I suppose I had spoken in the flat and affected accent of most expatriates. His accusation that my thinking was alien, strange, and indecent seemed invincible. I felt then, I feel now, that it was not the impropriety of my discovery but its explosiveness that disconcerted him, and that he had, in my absence, joined the ranks of those new men who feel that the truth is no longer usable in solving our dilemmas. He said good-bye, and one by one the others left, all on the same note—I had been away too long; I was out of touch with decency and common sense.

I returned to Europe a few days later. The plane for Orly was delayed, and I killed some time in the bar and then looked around for the men's room. The message this time was written on tile. "Bright Star!" I read, "would I were stedfast as thou art—Not in lone splendour hung aloft the night . . ." That was all. My flight was announced, and I sailed through the eaves of heaven back to the city of light.

 *Montraldo*

The first time I robbed Tiffany's, it was raining. I bought an imitation-diamond ring at a costume-jewelry place in the Forties. Then I walked up to Tiffany's in the rain and asked to look at rings. The clerk had a haughty manner. I looked at six or eight diamond rings. They began at eight hundred and went up to ten thousand. There was one priced at three thousand that looked to me like the paste in my pocket. I was examining this when an elderly woman—an old customer, I guessed—appeared on the other side of the counter. The clerk rushed over to greet her, and I switched rings. Then I called, "Thank you very much. I'll think it over." "Very well," the clerk said haughtily, and I went out of the store. It was as simple as pie. I walked down to the diamond market in the Forties and sold the ring for eighteen hundred. No questions were asked. Then I went to Thomas Cook and found that the Conte di Salvini was sailing for Genoa at five. This was in

August, and there was plenty of space on the eastbound crossing. I took a cabin in first class and was standing at the bar when she sailed. The bar was not officially open, of course, but the bar Jack gave me a martini in a tumbler to hold me until we got into international waters. The Salvini had an exceptionally percussive whistle, and you may have heard it if you were anywhere near midtown, although who ever is at five o'clock on an August afternoon?

That night I met Mrs. Winwar and her elderly husband at the horse races. He promptly got seasick, and we plunged into the marvelous skulduggery of illicit love. The passed notes, the phony telephone calls, the affected indifference, and what happened when we were behind the closed door of my cabin made my theft of a ring seem guileless. Mr. Winwar recovered in Gibraltar, but this only seemed like a challenge, and we carried on under his nose. We said good-bye in Genoa, where I bought a secondhand Fiat and started down the coast.

I got to Montraldo late one afternoon. I stopped there because I was tired of driving. There was a semicircular bay, set within high stone cliffs, and one of those beaches that are lined with cafés and bathing houses. There were two hotels, a Grand and a National, and I didn't care for either one of them, and a waiter in a café told me I could rent a room in the villa on the cliff. It could be reached, he said, either by a steep and curving road or by a flight of stone steps—one hundred and twenty-seven, I discovered later—that led from the back garden down into the village. I took my car up the curving road. The cliff was covered with rosemary, and the rosemary was covered with the village laundry, drying in the sun. There were signs on the door in five languages, saying that rooms were for rent. I rang, and a thickset, bellicose servant opened the door. I learned that her name was Assunta. I never saw any relaxation of her bellicosity. In church, when she plunged up the aisle to take Holy Communion, she looked as if she were going to knock the priest down and mess up the acolyte. She said I could have a room if I paid a week's rent in advance, and I had to pay her before I was allowed to cross the threshold.

The place was a ruin, but the whitewashed room she showed me into was in a little tower, and through a broken window the room had a broad view of the sea. The one luxury was a gas ring. There was no toilet, and there was no running water; the water I washed in had to be hauled out of a well in a leaky marmalade can. I was obviously the only guest. That first afternoon, while Assunta was praising the healthfulness of the sea air, I heard a querulous and elegant voice calling to us from the courtyard. I went down the stairs ahead of the servant, and introduced myself to an old woman standing by the well. She was short, frail, and animated, and spoke such a flowery Roman that I wondered if this wasn't a sort of cultural or social dust thrown into one's eyes to conceal the fact that her dress was ragged and dirty. "I see you have a gold wristwatch," she said. "I, too, have a gold wristwatch. We will have this in common."

The servant turned to her and said, "Go to the devil!"

"But it is a fact. The gentleman and I do both have gold wristwatches," the old lady said. "It will make us sympathetic."

"Bore," the servant said. "Rot in hell."

"Thank you, thank you, treasure of my house, light of my life," the old lady said, and made her way toward an open door.

The servant put her hands on her hips and screamed, "Witch! Frog! Pig!"

"Thank you, thank you, thank you infinitely," the old lady said, and went in at the door.

. . .

That night, at the café, I asked about the *signorina* and her servant, and the waiter was fully informed. The *signorina*, he said, came from a noble Roman family, from which she had been expelled because of a romantic and unsuitable love affair. She had lived as a hermit in Montraldo for fifty years. Assunta had been brought here from Rome to be her *donna di servizio*, but all she did for the old lady these days was to go into the village and buy her some bread and wine. She had robbed the old woman of all her possessions—she had even taken the bed from her room—and she now kept her a prisoner in the villa. Both the Grand Hotel and the National were luxurious and commodious. Why did I stay in such a place?

I stayed because of the view, because I had paid my rent in advance, and because I was curious about the eccentric old spinster and her cranky servant. They began quarreling early the next morning. Assunta opened up with obscenity and abuse. The *signorina* countered with elaborate sarcasm. It was a depressing performance. I wondered if the old lady was really a prisoner, and later in the morning, when I saw her alone in the courtyard, I asked her if she would like to drive with me to Tambura, the next village up the coast. She said, in her flowery Roman, that she would be delighted to join me. She wanted to have her watch, her gold watch, repaired. The watch was of great value and beauty and there was only one man she dared entrust it to. He was in Tambura. While we were talking, Assunta joined us.

"Why do you want to go to Tambura?" she asked the old lady.

"I want to have my gold watch repaired," the old lady said.

"You don't have a gold watch," Assunta said.

"That is true," the old lady said. "I no longer have a gold watch, but I used to have a gold watch. I used to have a gold watch, and I used to have a gold pencil."

"You can't go to Tambura to have your watch repaired if you don't have a watch," Assunta said.

"That is true, light of my life, treasure of my house," the old lady said, and she went in at her door.

I spent most of my time on the beach and in the cafés. The fortunes of the resort seemed to be middling. The waiters complained about business, but then they always do. The smell of the sea was riggish but unfresh, and I used to think with homesickness of the wild and magnificent beaches of my own country. Gay Head is, I know, sinking into the sea, but the sinkage at Montraldo seemed to be spiritual—as if the waves were eroding the vitality of that place. The sea was incandescent; the light was clear but not brilliant. The flavor of Montraldo, as I remember it, was immutable, intimate, depleted—everything I detest; for shouldn't the soul of man be as limpid and cutting as a diamond? The waves spoke in French or Italian—now and then a word of dialect—but they seemed to speak without force.

One afternoon a remarkably beautiful woman came down the beach, followed by a boy of about eight, I should say, and an Italian woman dressed in black—a maid. They carried sandwich bags from the Grand Hotel, and my guess was that the boy lived mostly in hotels. He was pitiful. The maid took some toys from an assortment she carried in a string bag. They seemed to be all wrong for his age. There was a sand bucket, a shovel, some molds, a whiffle ball, and an old-fashioned pair of water wings. I suspected that the mother, stretched out on a blanket with an American novel, was a divorcée, and that she would presently have a drink with me in the café. With this in mind, I got to my feet and offered to play whiffle ball with the boy. He was delighted to have some company, but he could neither throw nor catch a ball, and, making a guess at his tastes, I asked, with one eye on the mother, if he would like me to build him a sand castle. He would. I built a water moat, then an escarpment with curved stairs, a dry moat, a crenelated wall with cannon positions, and a cluster of round towers with parapets. I worked as if the impregnability of the place was a reality, and when it was completed I set flags, made of candy wrappers, flying from every tower. I thought naïvely that it was beautiful, and so did the boy, but when I called his mother's attention to my feat she said, "*Andiamo*." The maid gathered up the toys, and off they went, leaving me, a grown man in a strange country, with a sand castle.

At Montraldo, the high point of the day came at four, when there was a band concert. This was the largesse of the municipality. The bandstand was wooden, Turkish in inspiration, and weathered by the sea winds. The musicians sometimes wore uniforms, sometimes bathing suits, and their number varied from day to day, but they always played Dixieland. I don't think they were interested in the history of jazz. I just think they'd found some old arrangements in a trunk and were stuck with them. The music was comical, accelerated—they seemed to be playing for some ancient ballroom team. "Clarinet Marmalade," "China Boy," "Tiger Rag," "Careless Love"— how stirring it was to hear this old, old jazz explode in the salty air. The concert ended at five, when most of the musicians packed up their instruments and went out to sea with the sardine fleet and the bathers returned to the cafés and the village. Men, women, and children on a beach, band music, sea grass, and sandwich hampers remind me much more forcibly than classical landscapes of our legendary ties to paradise. So I would go up with the others to the café, where, one day, I befriended Lord and Lady Rockwell, who asked me for cocktails. You may wonder why I put these titles down so breathlessly, and the reason is that my father was a waiter.

He wasn't an ordinary waiter; he used to work at a dinner-dance spot in one of the big hotels. One night he lost his temper at a drunken brute, pushed his face into a plate of *cannelloni*, and left the premises. The union suspended him for three months, but he was, in a way, a hero, and when he went back to work they put him on the banquet shift, where he passed mushrooms to kings and presidents. He saw a lot of the world, but I sometimes wonder if the world ever saw much more of him than the sleeve of his red coat and his suave and handsome face, a little above the candlelight. It must have been like living in a world divided by a sheet of one-way glass. Sometimes I am reminded of him by those pages and guards in Shakespeare who come in from the left and stand at a door, establishing by their costumes the fact that this is Venice or Arden. You scarcely see their faces, they never speak a line; nor did my father, and when the after-dinner speeches began he would vanish like the pages on stage. I tell people that he was in the administrative end of the hotel business, but actually he was a waiter, a banquet waiter.

The Rockwells' party was large, and I left at about ten. A hot wind was blowing off the sea. I was later told that this was the sirocco. It was a desert wind, and so oppressive that I got up several times during the night to drink some mineral water. A boat offshore was sounding its foghorn. In the morning, it was both foggy and suffocating. While I was making some coffee, Assunta and the *signorina* began their morning quarrel. Assunta started off with the usual "Pig! Dog! Witch! Dirt of the streets!" Leaning from an open window, the whiskery old woman sent down her flowery replies: "Dear one. Beloved. Blessed one. Thank you, thank you." I stood in the door with my coffee, wishing they would schedule their disputes for some other time of day. The quarrel was suspended while the *signorina* came down the stairs to get her bread and wine. Then it started up again: "Witch! Frog! Frog of frogs! Witch of witches!," etc. The old lady countered with "Treasure! Light! Treasure of my house! Light of my life!," etc. Then there was a scuffle—a tug of war over the loaf of bread. I saw Assunta strike the old woman cruelly with the edge of her hand. She fell on the steps and began to moan "Aiee! Aieee!" Even these cries of pain seemed florid. I ran across the courtyard to where she lay in a disjointed heap. Assunta began to scream at me, "I am not culpable, I am not culpable!" The old lady was in great pain. "Please, *Signore*," she asked, "please find the priest for me!" I picked her up. She weighed no more than a child, and her clothing smelled of soil. I carried her up the stairs into a high-ceilinged room festooned with cobwebs and put her onto a couch. Assunta was on my heels, screaming, "I am not culpable!" Then I started down the one hundred and twenty-seven steps to the village.

The fog streamed through the air, and the African wind felt like a furnace draft. No one answered the door at the priest's house, but I found him in the church, sweeping the floor with a broom made of twigs. I was excited and impatient, and the more excited I became the more slow-moving was the priest. First, he had to put his broom in a closet. The closet door was warped and wouldn't shut, and he spent an unconscionable amount of time trying to close it. I finally went outside and waited on the porch. It took him half an hour to get collected, and then, instead of starting for the villa, we went down into the village to find an acolyte. Presently a young boy joined us, pulling on a soiled lace soutane, and we started up the stairs. The priest negotiated ten steps and then sat down to rest. I had time to smoke a cigarette. Then ten more steps and another rest, and when we were halfway up the stairs, I began to wonder if he would ever make it. His face had turned from red to purple, and the noises from his respiratory tract were harsh and desperate. We finally arrived at the door of the villa. The acolyte lit his censer. Then we made our way into that ruined place. The windows were open. There was sea fog in the air. The old woman was in great pain, but the notes of her voice remained genteel, as I expect they truly were. "She is my daughter," she said. "Assunta. She is my daughter, my child."

Then Assunta screamed, "Liar! Liar!"

"No, no, no," the old lady said, "you are my child, my only child. That is why I have cared for you all my life."

Assunta began to cry, and stamped down the stairs. From the window, I saw her crossing the courtyard. When the priest began to administer the last rites, I went out.

I kept a sort of vigil in the café. The church bells tolled at three, and a little later news came down from the villa that the *signorina* was dead. No one in the café seemed to suspect that they were anything but an eccentric old spinster and a cranky servant. At four o'clock the band concert opened up with "Tiger Rag." I moved that night from the villa to the Hotel National, and left Montraldo in the morning.

 *Three Stories*

I

The subject today will be the metaphysics of obesity, and I am the belly of a man named Lawrence Farnsworth. I am the body cavity between his diaphragm and his pelvic floor and I possess his viscera. I know you won't believe me, but if you'll buy a *cri de coeur* why not a *cri de ventre*? I play as large a part in his affairs as any other lights and vitals, and while I can't act independently he too is at the mercy of such disparate forces in his environment as money and starlight. We were born in the Middle West and he was educated in Chicago. He was on the track team (pole vault) and later on the diving team, two sports that made my existence dangerous and obscure. I did not discover myself until he was in his forties, when I was recognized by his doctor and his tailor. He stubbornly refused to grant me my rights and continued for almost a year to wear clothes that confined me harshly and caused me much soreness and pain. My one compensation was that I could unzip his fly at will.

I've often heard him say that, having spent the first half of his life running around behind an unruly bowsprit, he seemed damned to spend the rest of his life going around behind a belly that was as independent and capricious as his genitals. I have been, of course, in a position to observe his carnal sport, but I think I won't describe the thousands—or millions—of performances in which I have participated. I am, in spite of my reputation for grossness, truly visionary, and I would like to look past his gymnastics to their consequences, which, from what I hear, are often ecstatic. He seems to feel that his erotic life is an entry permit into what is truly beautiful in the world. Balling in a thunderstorm—any rain will do—is his idea of a total relationship. There have been complaints. I once heard a woman ask: "Will you never understand that there is more to life than sex and nature worship?" Once, when he exclaimed over the beauty of the stars his *belle amie* giggled. My open knowledge of the world is confined to the limited incidence of nakedness: bedrooms, showers, beaches, swimming pools, trysts, and sunbathing in the Antilles. The rest of my life is spent in a sort of purdah between his trousers and his shirts.

Having refused to admit my existence for a year or more, he finally had his trousers enlarged from thirty to thirty-four. When I had reached thirty-four inches and was striving for thirty-six his feelings about my existence became obsessive. The clash between what he had been and wanted to be and what he had become was serious. When people poked me with their fingers and made jokes about his Bay Window his forced laughter could not conceal his rage. He ceased to judge his friends on their wit and intelligence and began to judge them on their waistbands. Why was X so flat and why was Z, with a paunch of at least forty inches, contented with this state of affairs. When his friends stood his eye dropped swiftly from their smiles to their middles. We went one night to Yankee

Stadium to see a ball game. He had begun to enjoy himself when he noticed that the right fielder had a good thirty-six inches. The other fielders and the basemen passed but the pitcher—an older man—had a definite bulge—and two of the umpires—when they took off their guards—were disgusting. So was the catcher. When he realized that he was not watching a ball game—that because of my influence he was unable to watch a ball game—we left. This was at the top of the fourth. A day or two later he began what was to be a year or a year and a half of hell.

We started with a diet that emphasized water and hard-boiled eggs. He lost ten pounds in a week but he lost it all in the wrong places, and while my existence was imperiled I survived. The diet set up some metabolic disturbance that damaged his teeth, and he gave this up at his doctor's suggestion and joined a health club. Three times a week I was tormented on an electric bicycle and a rowing machine and then a masseur would knead me and strike me loudly and cruelly with the flat of his hand. He then bought a variety of elastic underpants or girdles that meant to disguise or dismiss me, and while they gave me great pain they only challenged my invincibility. When they were removed in the evening I reinstated myself amply in the world I so much love. Soon after this he bought a contraption that was guaranteed to destroy me. This was a pair of gold-colored plastic shorts that could be inflated by a hand pump. The acidity of the secretions I had to refine informed me of how painful and ridiculous he felt. When the shorts were inflated he read from a book of directions and performed some gymnastics. This was the worst pain to be inflicted on me so far, and when the exercises were finished my various parts were so abnormally cramped and knotted that we spent a sleepless night.

By this time I had come to recognize two facts that guaranteed my survival. The first was his detestation of solitary exercise. He liked games well enough but he did not like gymnastics. Each morning he would go to the bathroom and touch his toes ten times. His buttocks (there's another story) scraped the washbasin and his forehead grazed the toilet seat. I knew from the secretions that came my way that this experience was spiritually crushing. Later he moved to the country for the summer and took up jogging and weight lifting. While lifting weights he learned to count in Japanese and Russian, hoping to give this performance some dignity, but he was not successful. Both jogging and weight lifting embarrassed him intensely. The second factor in my favor was his conviction that we lead a simple life. "I really lead a very simple life," he often said. If this were so I would have no chance for prominence, but there is, I think, no first-class restaurant in Europe, Asia, Africa, or the British Isles to which I have not been taken and asked to perform. He often says so. Going after a dish of crickets in Tokyo he gave me a friendly pat and said: "Do your best, man." So long as he considers this to be a simple life my place in the world is secure. When I fail him it is not through malice or intent. After a Homeric dinner with fourteen entrées in southern Russia we spent a night together in the bathroom. This was in Tbilisi. I seemed to be threatening his life. It was three in the morning. He was crying with pain. He was weeping, and perhaps I know more than any other part of his physique about the true loneliness of this man. "Go away," he shouted at me, "go away." What could be more pitiful and absurd than a naked man at the dog hour in a strange country casting out his vitals. We went to the window to hear the wind in the trees. "Oh, I should have paid more attention to spiritual things," he shouted.

If I were the belly of a secret agent or a reigning prince my role in the clash of time wouldn't have been any different. I represent time more succinctly than any scarecrow with a scythe. Why should so simple a force as time—told accurately by the clocks in his house—cause him to groan and swear? Did he feel that some specious youthfulness was his principle, his only lure? I know that I reminded him of the pain he suffered in his relationship to his father. His father retired at fifty-five and spent the rest of his life polishing stones, gardening, and trying to learn conversational French from records. He had been a limber and an athletic man, but like his son he had been overtaken in the middle of the way by an independent abdomen. He seemed, like his son, to have no capacity to age and fatten gracefully. His paunch, his abdomen seemed to break his spirit. His abdomen led him to stoop, to walk clumsily, to sigh, and to have his trousers enlarged. His abdomen seemed like some precursor of the Angel of Death, and was Farnsworth, touching his toes in the bathroom each morning, struggling with the same angel?

Then there was the year we traveled. I don't know what drove him, but we went around the world three times in twelve months. He may have thought that travel would heighten his metabolism and diminish my importance. I won't go into the hardships of safety belts and a chaotic eating schedule. We saw all the usual places as well as Nairobi, Malagasy, Mauritius, Bali, New Guinea, New Caledonia, and New Zealand. We saw Madang, Goroka, Lee, Rabaul, Fiji, Reykjavík, Thingvellir, Akureyri, Narsarssuak, Kagsiarauk, Bukhara, Irkutsk, Ulan Bator, and the Gobi Desert. Then there were the Galápagos, Patagonia, the Mato Grosso jungle, and of course the Seychelles and the Amirantes.

It ended or was resolved one night at Passetto's. He began the meal with figs and Parma ham and with this he ate two

rolls and butter. After this he had *spaghetti carbonara,* a steak
with fried potatoes, a serving of frogs' legs, a whole *spigola*
roasted in paper, some chicken breasts, a salad with an oil
dressing, three kinds of cheese, and a thick *zabaglione.* Halfway through the meal he had to give me some leeway, but he
was not resentful and I felt that victory might be in sight.
When he ordered the *zabaglione* I knew that I had won or
that we had arrived at a sensible truce. He was not trying to
conceal, dismiss, or forget me and his secretions were bland.
Leaving the table he had to give me another two inches, so
that walking across the piazza I could feel the night wind and
hear the fountains, and we've lived happily together ever since.

II

Marge Littleton would, in the long-gone days of Freudian
jargon, have been thought maternal although she was no
more maternal than you or you. What would have been
meant was a charming softness in her voice and her manner
and she smelled like a summer's day, or perhaps it is a summer's
day that smells like such a woman. She was a regular church-
goer, and I always felt that her devotions were more profound
than most, although it is impossible to speculate on anything so
intimate. She was on the liturgical side, hewing to the Book of
Common Prayer and avoiding sermons whenever possible. She
was not a native, of course—the last native along with the last
cow died twenty years ago—and I don't remember where she
or her husband came from. He was bald. They had three chil-

dren and lived a scrupulously unexceptional life until one morning in the fall.

It was after Labor Day, a little windy. Leaves could be seen falling outside the windows. The family had breakfast in the kitchen. Marge had baked johnnycake. "Good morning, Mrs. Littleton," her husband said, kissing her on the brow and patting her backside. His voice, his gesture seemed to have the perfect equilibrium of love. I don't know what virulent critics of the family would say about the scene. Were the Littletons making for themselves, by contorting their passions into an acceptable social image, a sort of prison, or did they chance to be a man and woman whose pleasure in one another was tender, robust, and invincible? From what I know it was an exceptional marriage. Never having been married myself I may be unduly susceptible to the element of buffoonery in holy matrimony, but isn't it true that when some couple celebrates their tenth or fifteenth anniversary they seem far from triumphant? In fact they seem duped while dirty Uncle Harry, the rake, seems to wear the laurels. But with the Littletons one felt that they might live together with intelligence and ardor—giving and taking until death did them part.

On that particular Saturday morning he planned to go shopping. After breakfast he made a list of what they needed from the hardware store. A gallon of white acrylic paint, a four-inch brush, picture hooks, a spading fork, oil for the lawn mower. The children went along with him. They went, not to the village, which, like so many others, lay dying, but to a crowded and fairly festive shopping center on Route 64. He gave the children money for Cokes. When they returned the southbound traffic was heavy. It was as I say after Labor Day, and many of the cars were towing portable houses, campers, sailboats, motorboats, and trailers. This long procession of vehicles and domestic portables seemed not the spectacle of a people returning from their vacations but rather like a tragic evacuation of some great city or state. A car carrier, trying to pass an exceptionally bulky mobile home, crashed into the Littletons and killed them all. I didn't go to the funeral but one of our neighbors described it to me. "There she stood at the edge of the grave. She didn't cry. She looked very beautiful and serene. She had to watch four coffins, one after the other, lowered into the ground. Four."

She didn't go away. People asked her to dinner, of course, but in such an intensely domesticated community the single are inevitably neglected. A month or so after the accident the local paper announced that the State Highway Commission would widen Route 64 from a four-lane to an eight-lane highway. We organized a committee for the preservation of the community and raised ten thousand dollars for legal fees. Marge Littleton was very active. We had meetings nearly every week. We met in parish houses, courtrooms, high schools, and houses. In the beginning these meetings were very emotional. Mrs. Pinkham once cried. She wept. "I've worked sixteen years on my pink room and now they're going to tear it down." She was led out of the meeting, a truly bereaved woman. We chartered a bus and went to the state capital. We marched down 64 one rainy Sunday with a motorcycle escort. I don't suppose we were more than thirty and we straggled. We carried picket signs. I remember Marge. Some people seem born with a congenital gift for protest and a talent for carrying picket signs, but this was not Marge. She carried a large sign that said STOP GASOLINE ALLEY. She seemed very embarrassed. When the march disbanded I said good-bye to her on a knoll above the highway. I remember the level gaze she gave to the lines of traffic, rather, I guess, as the widows of Nantucket must have regarded the sea.

When we had spent our ten thousand dollars without any results our meetings were less and less frequent and very poorly attended. Only three people, including the speaker, showed up for the last. The highway was widened, demolishing six houses and making two uninhabitable, although the owners got no compensation. Several wells were destroyed by the blasting. After our committee was disbanded I saw very little of Marge. Someone told me she had gone abroad. When she returned she was followed by a charming young Roman named Pietro Montani. They were married.

Marge displayed her gifts for married happiness with Pietro although he was very unlike her first husband. He was handsome, witty, and substantial—he represented a firm that manufactured innersoles—but he spoke the worst English I have ever heard. You could talk with him and drink with him and laugh with him but other than this it was almost impossible to communicate with him. It didn't really matter. She seemed very happy and it was a pleasant house to visit. They had been married no more than two months when Pietro, driving a convertible down 64, was decapitated by a crane.

She buried Pietro with the others but she stayed on in the house on Twin-Rock Road, where one could hear the battlefield noises of industrial traffic. I think she got a job. One saw her on the trains. Three weeks after Pietro's death a twenty-four wheel, eighty-ton truck, northbound on Route 64 for reasons that were never ascertained, veered into the southbound lane demolishing two cars and killing their four passengers. The truck then rammed into a granite abutment there, fell on its side, and caught fire. The police and the fire department were there at once, but the freight was combustible and the fire was not extinguished until three in the morning. All traffic on Route 64 was rerouted. The women's auxiliary of the fire department served coffee.

Two weeks later at 8:00 P.M. another twenty-four wheel truck with a load of cement block went out of control at the same place, crossed the southbound lane, and felled four full-grown trees before it collided with the abutment. The impact of the collision was so violent that two feet of granite were sheered off the wall. There was no fire, but the two drivers were so badly crushed by the collision that they had to be identified by their dental work.

On November third at 8:30 P.M. Lt. Dominic DeSisto reported that a man in work clothes ran into the front office. He seemed hysterical, drugged, or drunk and claimed to have been shot. He was, according to Lieutenant DeSisto, so incoherent that it was some time before he could explain what had happened. Driving north on 64, at about the same place where the other trucks had gone out of control, a rifle bullet had smashed the left window of his cab, missed the driver, and smashed the right window. The intended victim was Joe Langston of Baldwin, South Carolina. The lieutenant examined the truck and verified the broken windows. He and Langston drove in a squad car back to where the shot had been fired. On the right side of the road there was a little hill of granite with some soil covering. When the highway had been widened the hill had been blasted in two and the knoll on the right corresponded to the abutment that had killed the other drivers. DeSisto examined the hill. The grass on the knoll was trampled and there were two cigarette butts on the ground. Langston was taken to the hospital, suffering from shock. The hill was put under surveillance for the next month, but the police force was understaffed and it was a boring beat to sit alone on the hill from dusk until midnight. As soon as surveillance was stopped a fourth oversized truck went out of control. This time the truck veered to the right, took down a dozen trees, and drove into a narrow but precipitous valley. The driver, when the police got to him, was dead. He had been shot.

In December Marge married a rich widower and moved to North Salem, where there is only one two-lane highway and where the sound of traffic is as faint as the roaring of a shell.

III

He took his aisle seat—32—in the 707 for Rome. The plane was not quite full and there was an empty seat between him and the occupant of the port seat. This was taken, he was pleased to see, by an exceptionally good-looking woman— not young, but neither was he. She was wearing perfume, a dark dress, and jewelry and she seemed to belong to that part of the world in which he moved most easily. "Good evening," he said, settling himself. She didn't reply. She made a discouraging humming noise and raised a paperback book to the front of her face. He looked for the title but this she concealed with her hands. He had met shy women on planes before—infrequently, but he had met them. He supposed they were understandably wary of lushes, mashers, and bores. He shook out a copy of *The Manchester Guardian*. He had noticed that conservative newspapers sometimes inspired confidence in the shy. If one read the editorials, the sports page, and especially the financial section shy strangers would sometimes be ready for a conversation. The plane took off, the smoking sign went dark, and he took out a gold cigarette case and a gold lighter. They

were not flashy, but they were gold. "Do you mind if I
smoke?" he asked. "Why should I?" she asked. She did not
look in his direction. "Some people do," he said, lighting his
cigarette. She was nearly as beautiful as she was unfriendly,
but why should she be so cold? They would be side by side for
nine hours, and it was only sensible to count on at least a little
conversation. Did he remind her of someone she disliked, someone who had wounded her? He was bathed, shaved, correctly
dressed, and accustomed to making friends. Perhaps she was an
unhappy woman who disliked the world, but when the stewardess came by to take their drink orders the smile she gave the
young stranger was dazzling and open. This so cheered him
that he smiled himself, but when she saw that he was trespassing
on a communication that was aimed at someone else she turned
on him, scowled, and went back to her book. The stewardess
brought him a double martini and his companion a sherry. He
supposed that his strong drink might increase her uneasiness,
but he had to take that chance. She went on reading. If he
could only find the title of the book, he thought, he would
have a foot in the door. Harold Robbins, Dostoevsky, Philip
Roth, Emily Dickinson—anything would help. "May I ask
what you're reading?" he said politely. "No," she said.

When the stewardess brought their dinners he passed her
tray across the empty seat. She did not thank him. He settled
down to eat, to feed, to enjoy this simple habit. The meal was
unusually bad and he said so. "One can't be too particular
under the circumstances," she said. He thought he heard a
trace of warmth in her voice. "Salt might help," she said, "but
they neglected to give me any salt. Could I trouble you for
yours?" "Oh certainly," he said. Things were definitely looking up. He opened his salt container and in passing it to her a
little salt spilled on the rug. "I'm afraid the bad luck will be

yours," she said. This was not said at all lightly. She salted her
cutlet and ate everything on her tray. Then she went on reading
the book with the concealed title. She would sooner or later
have to use the toilet, he knew, and then he could read the title
of the book, but when she did go to the stern of the plane she
carried the book with her.

The screen for the film was lowered. Unless a picture was
exceptionally interesting he never rented sound equipment. He
had found that lipreading and guesswork gave the picture an
added dimension, and anyhow the dialogue was usually offen-
sively banal. His neighbor rented equipment and seemed to enjoy herself heartily. She had a lovely musical laugh and
communicated with the actors on the screen as she had communicated with the stewardess and as she had refused to
communicate with her neighbor. The sun rose as they approached the Alps, although the film was not over. Here and
there the brightness of an alpine morning could be seen
through the cracks in the drawn shades, but while they sailed
over Mont Blanc and the Matterhorn the characters on the
screen relentlessly pursued their script. There was a parade, a
chase, a reconciliation, an ending. His companion, still carrying her mysterious book, retired to the stern again and returned
wearing a sort of mobcap, her face heavily covered with some
white unguent. She adjusted her pillow and blanket and arranged herself for sleep. "Sweet dreams," he said, daringly.
She sighed.

He never slept on planes. He went up to the galley and had
a whiskey. The stewardess was pretty and talkative and she
told him about her origins, her schedule, her fiancé, and her
problems with passengers who suffered from flight fear. Beyond the Alps they began to lose altitude and he saw the
Mediterranean from the port and had another whiskey. He saw

Elba, Giglio, and the yachts in the harbor at Porte Ercole
where he could see the villas of his friends. He could remember
coming into Nantucket so many years ago. They used to line
the port railing and shout: "Oh, the Perrys are here and the
Saltons and the Greenoughs." It was partly genuine, partly
show. When he returned to his seat his companion had removed her mobcap and her unguent. Her beauty in the light
of morning was powerful. He could not diagnose what he
found so compelling—nostalgia, perhaps—but her features, her
pallor, the set of her eyes, all corresponded to his sense of
beauty. "Good morning," he said, "did you sleep well?" She
frowned, she seemed to find this impertinent. "Does one ever,"
she asked on a rising note. She put her mysterious book into a
handbag with a zipper and gathered her things. When they
landed at Fiumicino he stood aside to let her pass and followed
her down the aisle. He went behind her through the passport,
emigrant, and health check and joined her at the place where
you claim your bags.

But look, look. Why does he point out her bag to the
porter and why, when they both have their bags, does he follow her out to the cab stand, where he bargains with a driver
for the trip into Rome? Why does he join her in the cab? Is he
the undiscourageable masher that she dreaded? No, no. He is
her husband, she is his wife, the mother of his children, and a
woman he has worshiped passionately for nearly thirty years.

The Geometry
of Love

It was one of those rainy late afternoons when the toy department of Woolworth's on Fifth Avenue is full of women who appear to have been taken in adultery and who are now shopping for a present to carry home to their youngest child. On this particular afternoon there were eight or ten of them— comely, fragrant, and well dressed—but with the pained air of women who have recently been undone by some cad in a midtown hotel room and who are now on their way home to the embraces of a tender child. It was Charlie Mallory, walking away from the hardware department, where he had bought a screwdriver, who reached this conclusion. There was no morality involved. He hit on this generalization mostly to give the lassitude of a rainy afternoon some intentness and color. Things were slow at his office. He had spent the time since lunch repairing a filing cabinet. Thus the screwdriver. Having settled on this conjecture, he looked more closely into the faces of the women and seemed to find there some affirmation of his fantasy. What but the engorgements and chagrins of adultery could have left them all looking so spiritual, so tearful? Why should they sigh so deeply as they fingered the playthings of innocence? One of the women wore a fur coat that looked like a coat he had bought his wife, Mathilda, for Christmas. Looking more closely, he saw that it was not only Mathilda's coat, it was Mathilda. "Why, Mathilda," he cried, "what in the world are you doing here?"

She raised her head from the wooden duck she had been studying. Slowly, slowly, the look of chagrin on her face shaded into anger and scorn. "I detest being spied upon," she said. Her voice was strong, and the other women shoppers looked up, ready for anything.

Mallory was at a loss. "But I'm not spying on you, darling," he said. "I only—"

"I can't think of anything more despicable," she said, "than following people through the streets." Her mien and her voice were operatic, and her audience was attentive and rapidly being enlarged by shoppers from the hardware and garden-furniture sections. "To hound an innocent woman through the streets is the lowest, sickest, and most vile of occupations."

"But, darling, I just happened to be here."

Her laughter was pitiless. "You just happened to be hanging around the toy department at Woolworth's? Do you expect me to believe that?"

"I was in the hardware department," he said, "but it doesn't really matter. Why don't we have a drink together and take an early train?"

"I wouldn't drink or travel with a spy," she said. "I am going to leave this store now, and if you follow or harass me in any way, I shall have you arrested by the police and thrown into jail." She picked up and paid for the wooden duck and regally ascended the stairs. Mallory waited a few minutes and then walked back to his office.

Mallory was a free-lance engineer, and his office was empty that afternoon—his secretary had gone to Capri. The telephone-answering service had no messages for him. There was no mail. He was alone. He seemed not so much unhappy as stunned. It was not that he had lost his sense of reality but that the reality he observed had lost its fitness and symmetry. How could he apply reason to the slapstick encounter in Woolworth's, and yet how could he settle for unreason? Forgetfulness was a course of action he had tried before, but he could not forget Mathilda's ringing voice and the bizarre scenery of the toy department. Dramatic misunderstandings with Mathilda were common, and he usually tackled them willingly, trying to decipher the chain of contingencies that had detonated the scene. This afternoon he was discouraged. The encounter seemed to resist diagnosis. What could he do? Should he consult a psychiatrist, a marriage counselor, a minister? Should he jump out of the window? He went to the window with this in mind.

It was still overcast and rainy, but not yet dark. Traffic was slow. He watched below him as a station wagon passed, then a convertible, a moving van, and a small truck advertising Euclid's Dry Cleaning and Dyeing. The great name reminded him of the right-angled triangle, the principles of geometric analysis, and the doctrine of proportion for both commensurables and incommensurables. What he needed was a new form of ratiocination, and Euclid might do. If he could make a geometric analysis of his problems, mightn't he solve them, or at least create an atmosphere of solution? He got a slide rule and took the simple theorem that if two sides of a triangle are equal, the angles opposite these sides are equal; and the converse theorem that if two angles of a triangle are equal, the sides opposite them will be equal. He drew a line to represent Mathilda and what he knew about her to be relevant. The base of the triangle would be his two children, Randy and Priscilla. He, of course, would make up the third side. The most critical element in Mathilda's line—that which would threaten to make her angle unequal to Randy and Priscilla's—was the fact that she had recently taken a phantom lover.

This was a common imposture among the housewives of Remsen Park, where they lived. Once or twice a week, Mathilda would dress in her best, put on some French perfume and a fur coat, and take a late-morning train to the city. She sometimes lunched with a friend, but she lunched more often alone in one of those French restaurants in the sixties that accommodate single women. She usually drank a cocktail or had a half-bottle of wine. Her intention was to appear dissipated, mysterious—a victim of love's bitter riddle—but should a stranger give her the eye, she would go into a paroxysm of shyness, recalling, with something like panic, her lovely home, her fresh-faced children, and the begonias in her flower bed. In the afternoon, she went either to a matinee or a foreign movie. She preferred strenuous themes that would leave her emotionally exhausted—or, as she put it to herself, "emptied." Coming home on a late train, she would appear peaceful and sad. She often wept while she cooked the supper, and if Mallory asked what her trouble was, she would merely sigh. He was briefly suspicious, but walking up Madison Avenue one afternoon he saw her, in her furs, eating a sandwich at a lunch counter, and concluded that the pupils of her eyes were dilated not by amorousness but by the darkness of a movie theater. It was a harmless and a common imposture, and might even, with some forced charity, be thought of as useful.

The line formed by these elements, then, made an angle with the line representing his children, and the single fact *here* was that he loved them. He loved them! No amount of ignominy or venom could make parting from them imaginable. As he thought of them, they seemed to be the furniture of his soul, its lintel and rooftree.

The line representing himself, he knew, would be most prone to miscalculations. He thought himself candid, healthy, and knowledgeable (who else could remember so much Euclid?), but waking in the morning, feeling useful and innocent, he had only to speak to Mathilda to find his usefulness and his innocence squandered. Why should his ingenuous commitments to life seem to harass the best of him? Why should he, wandering through the toy department, be calumniated as a Peeping Tom? His triangle might give him the answer, he thought, and in a sense it did. The sides of the triangle, determined by the relevant information, were equal, as were the angles opposite these sides. Suddenly he felt much less bewildered, happier, more hopeful and magnanimous. He thought, as one does two or three times a year, that he was beginning a new life.

Coming home on the train, he wondered if he could make a geometrical analogy for the boredom of a commuters' local, the stupidities in the evening paper, the rush to the parking lot. Mathilda was in the small dining room, setting the table, when he returned. Her opening gun was meant to be disabling. "Pinkerton fink," she said. "Gumshoe." While he heard her words, he heard them without anger, anxiety, or frustration. They seemed to fall short of where he stood. How calm he felt, how happy. Even Mathilda's angularity seemed touching and lovable; this wayward child in the family of man. "Why do you look so happy?" his children asked. "Why do you look so happy, Daddy?" Presently, almost everyone would say the same. "How Mallory has changed. How well Mallory looks. Lucky Mallory!"

The next night, Mallory found a geometry text in the attic and refreshed his knowledge. The study of Euclid put him into a compassionate and tranquil frame of mind, and illuminated, among other things, that his thinking and feeling had recently been crippled by confusion and despair. He knew that what he thought of as his discovery could be an illusion, but the practical advantages remained his. He felt much better. He felt that he had corrected the distance between his reality and those realities that pounded at his spirit. He might not, had he possessed any philosophy or religion, have needed geometry, but the religious observances in his neighborhood seemed to him boring and threadbare, and he had no disposition for philosophy. Geometry served him beautifully for the metaphysics of understood pain. The principal advantage was that he could regard, once he had put them into linear terms, Mathilda's moods and discontents with ardor and compassion. He was not a victor, but he was wonderfully safe from being victimized. As he continued with his study and his practice, he discovered that the rudenesses of headwaiters, the damp souls of clerks, and the scurrilities of traffic policemen could not touch his tranquillity, and that these oppressors, in turn, sensing his strength, were less rude, damp, and scurrilous. He was able to carry the conviction of innocence, with which he woke each morning, well into the day. He thought of writing a book about his discovery: *Euclidean Emotion: The Geometry of Sentiment.*

The Geometry of Love

At about this time he had to go to Chicago. It was an overcast day, and he took the train. Waking a little after dawn, all usefulness and innocence, he looked out the window of his bedroom at a coffin factory, used-car dumps, shanties, weedy playing fields, pigs fattening on acorns, and in the distance the monumental gloom of Gary. The tedious and melancholy scene had the power over his spirit of a show of human stupidity. He had never applied his theorem to landscapes, but he discovered that, by translating the components of the moment into a parallelogram, he was able to put the discouraging countryside away from him until it seemed harmless, practical, and even charming. He ate a hearty breakfast and did a good day's work. It was a day that needed no geometry. One of his associates in Chicago asked him to dinner. It was an invitation that he felt he could not refuse, and he showed up at half past six at a little brick house in a part of the city with which he was unfamiliar. Even before the door opened, he felt that he was going to need Euclid.

His hostess, when she opened the door, had been crying. She held a drink in her hand. "He's in the cellar," she sobbed, and went into a small living room without telling Mallory where the cellar was or how to get there. He followed her into the living room. She had dropped to her hands and knees, and was tying a tag to the leg of a chair. Most of the furniture, Mallory noticed, was tagged. The tags were printed: CHICAGO STORAGE WAREHOUSE. Below this she had written: "Property of Helen Fells McGowen." McGowen was his friend's name. "I'm not going to leave the s.o.b. a thing," she sobbed. "Not a stick."

"Hi, Mallory," said McGowen, coming through the kitchen. "Don't pay any attention to her. Once or twice a year she gets sore and puts tags on all the furniture, and claims she's going to put it in storage and take a furnished room and work at Marshall Field's."

"You don't know *anything*," she said.

"What's new?" McGowen asked.

"Lois Mitchell just telephoned. Harry got drunk and put the kitten in the blender."

"Is she coming over?"

"Of course."

The doorbell rang. A disheveled woman with wet cheeks came in. "Oh, it was awful," she said. "The children were watching. It was their little kitten and they loved it. I wouldn't have minded so much if the children hadn't been watching."

"Let's get out of here," McGowen said, turning back to the kitchen. Mallory followed him through the kitchen, where there were no signs of dinner, down some stairs into a cellar furnished with a ping-pong table, a television set, and a bar. He got Mallory a drink. "You see, Helen used to be rich," McGowen said. "It's one of her difficulties. She came from very rich people. Her father had a chain of Laundromats that reached from here to Denver. He introduced live entertainment in Laundromats. Folk singers. Combos. Then the Musicians' Union ganged up on him, and he lost the whole thing overnight. And she knows that I fool around but if I wasn't promiscuous, Mallory, I wouldn't be true to myself. I mean, I used to make out with that Mitchell dame upstairs. The one with the kitten. She's great. You want her, I can fix it up. She'll do anything for me. I usually give her a little something. Ten bucks or a bottle of whiskey. One Christmas I gave her a bracelet. You see, her husband has this suicide thing. He keeps taking sleeping pills, but they always pump him out in time. Once, he tried to hang himself—"

"I've got to go," Mallory said.

"Stick around, stick around," McGowen said. "Let me sweeten your drink."

"I've really got to go," Mallory said. "I've got a lot of work to do."

"But you haven't had anything to eat," McGowen said. "Stick around and I'll heat up some gurry."

"There isn't time," Mallory said. "I've got a lot to do." He went upstairs without saying good-bye. Mrs. Mitchell had gone, but his hostess was still tying tags onto the furniture. He let himself out and took a cab back to his hotel.

He got out his slide rule and, working on the relation between the volume of a cone and that of its circumscribed prism, tried to put Mrs. McGowen's drunkenness and the destiny of the Mitchells' kitten into linear terms. Oh, Euclid, be with me now! What did Mallory want? He wanted radiance, beauty, and order, no less; he wanted to rationalize the image of Mr. Mitchell, hanging by the neck. Was Mallory's passionate detestation of squalor fastidious and unmanly? Was he wrong to look for definitions of good and evil, to believe in the inalienable power of remorse, the beauty of shame? There was a vast number of imponderables in the picture, but he tried to hold his equation to the facts of the evening, and this occupied him until past midnight, when he went to sleep. He slept well.

The Chicago trip had been a disaster as far as the Mc-Gowens went, but financially it had been profitable, and the Mallorys decided to take a trip, as they usually did whenever they were flush. They flew to Italy and stayed in a small hotel near Sperlonga where they had stayed before. Mallory was very happy and needed no Euclid for the ten days they spent on the coast. They went to Rome before flying home and, on their last day, went to the Piazza del Popolo for lunch. They ordered lobster, and were laughing, drinking, and cracking shells with their teeth when Mathilda became melancholy. She let out a sob, and Mallory realized that he was going to need Euclid.

Now Mathilda was moody, but that afternoon seemed to promise Mallory that he might, by way of groundwork and geometry, isolate the components of her moodiness. The restaurant seemed to present a splendid field for investigation. The place was fragrant and orderly. The other diners were decent Italians, all of them strangers, and he didn't imagine they had it in their power to make her as miserable as she plainly was. She had enjoyed her lobster. The linen was white, the silver polished, the waiter civil. Mallory examined the place— the flowers, the piles of fruit, the traffic in the square outside the window—and he could find in all of this no source for the sorrow and bitterness in her face. "Would you like an ice or some fruit?" he asked.

"If I want anything, I'll order it myself," she said, and she did. She summoned the waiter, ordered an ice and some coffee for herself, throwing Mallory a dark look. When Mallory had paid the check, he asked her if she wanted a cab. "What a stupid idea," she said, frowning with disgust, as if he had suggested squandering their savings account or putting their children on the stage.

They walked back to their hotel, Indian file. The light was brilliant, the heat was intense, and it seemed as if the streets of Rome had always been hot and would always be, world without end. Was it the heat that had changed her humor? "Does the heat bother you, dear?" he asked, and she turned and said, "You make me sick." He left her in the hotel lobby and went to a café.

He worked out his problems with a slide rule on the back

of a menu. When he returned to the hotel, she had gone out, but she came in at seven and began to cry as soon as she entered the room. The afternoon's geometry had proved to him that her happiness, as well as his and that of his children, suffered from some capricious, unfathomable, and submarine course of emotion that wound mysteriously through her nature, erupting with turbulence at intervals that had no regularity and no discernible cause. "I'm sorry, my darling," he said. "What is the matter?"

"No one in this city understands English," she said, "absolutely no one. I got lost and I must have asked fifteen people the way back to the hotel, but no one understood me." She went into the bathroom and slammed the door, and he sat at the window—calm and happy—watching the traverse of a cloud shaped exactly like a cloud, and then the appearance of that brassy light that sometimes fills up the skies of Rome just before dark.

Mallory had to go back to Chicago a few days after they returned from Italy. He finished his business in a day—he avoided McGowen—and got the four-o'clock train. At about four-thirty he went up to the club car for a drink, and seeing the mass of Gary in the distance, repeated that theorem that had corrected the angle of his relationship to the Indiana landscape. He ordered a drink and looked out of the window at Gary. There was nothing to be seen. He had, through some miscalculation, not only rendered Gary powerless; he had lost Gary. There was no rain, no fog, no sudden dark to account for the fact that, to his eyes, the windows of the club car were vacant. Indiana had disappeared. He turned to a woman on his left and asked, "That's Gary, isn't it?"

"Sure," she said. "What's the matter? Can't you see?"

An isosceles triangle took the sting out of her remark, but there was no trace of any of the other towns that followed. He went back to his bedroom, a lonely and a frightened man. He buried his face in his hands, and, when he raised it, he could clearly see the lights of the grade crossings and the little towns, but he had never applied his geometry to these.

It was perhaps a week later that Mallory was taken sick. His secretary—she had returned from Capri—found him unconscious on the floor of the office. She called an ambulance. He was operated on and listed as in critical condition. It was ten days after his operation before he could have a visitor, and the first, of course, was Mathilda. He had lost ten inches of his intestinal tract, and there were tubes attached to both his arms. "Why, you're looking marvelous," Mathilda exclaimed, turning the look of shock and dismay on her face inward and settling for an expression of absentmindedness. "And it's such a pleasant room. Those yellow walls. If you have to be sick, I guess it's best to be sick in New York. Remember that awful country hospital where I had the children?" She came to rest, not in a chair, but on the windowsill. He reminded himself that he had never known a love that could quite anneal the divisive power of pain; that could bridge the distance between the quick and the infirm. "Everything at the house is fine and dandy," she said. "Nobody seems to miss you."

Never having been gravely ill before, he had no way of anticipating the poverty of her gifts as a nurse. She seemed to resent the fact that he was ill, but her resentment was, he thought, a clumsy expression of love. She had never been adroit at concealment, and she could not conceal the fact that she considered his collapse to be selfish. "You're so lucky," she said. "I mean you're so lucky it happened in New York. You have the best doctors and the best nurses, and this must be one of the best hospitals in the world. You've nothing to worry about, really. Everything's done for you. I just wish that once in my life I could get into bed for a week or two and be waited on."

It was his Mathilda speaking, his beloved Mathilda, unsparing of herself in displaying that angularity, that legitimate self-interest that no force of love could reason or soften. This was she, and he appreciated the absence of sentimentality with which she appeared. A nurse came in with a bowl of clear soup on a tray. She spread a napkin under his chin and prepared to feed him, since he could not move his arms. "Oh, let me do it, let me do it." Mathilda said. "It's the least I can do." It was the first hint of the fact that she was in any way involved in what was, in spite of the yellow walls, a tragic scene. She took the bowl of soup and the spoon from the nurse. "Oh, how good that smells," she said. "I have half a mind to eat it myself. Hospital food is supposed to be dreadful, but this place seems to be an exception." She held a spoonful of the broth up to his lips and then, through no fault of her own, spilled the bowl of broth over his chest and bedclothes.

She rang for the nurse and then vigorously rubbed at a spot on her skirt. When the nurse began the lengthy and complicated business of changing his bed linen, Mathilda looked at her watch and saw that it was time to go. "I'll stop in tomorrow," she said. "I'll tell the children how well you look."

It was his Mathilda, and this much he understood, but when she had gone he realized that understanding might not get him through another such visit. He definitely felt that the convalescence of his guts had suffered a setback. She might even hasten his death. When the nurse had finished changing him and had fed him a second bowl of soup, he asked her to get the slide rule and notebook out of the pocket of his suit. He worked out a simple, geometrical analogy between his love for Mathilda and his fear of death.

It seemed to work. When Mathilda came at eleven the next day, he could hear her and see her, but she had lost the power to confuse. He had corrected her angle. She was dressed for her phantom lover and she went on about how well he looked and how lucky he was. She did point out that he needed a shave. When she had left, he asked the nurse if he could have a barber. She explained that the barber came only on Wednesdays and Fridays, and that the male nurses were all out on strike. She brought him a mirror, a razor, and some soap, and he saw his face then for the first time since his collapse. His emaciation forced him back to geometry, and he tried to equate the voracity of his appetite, the boundlessness of his hopes, and the frailty of his carcass. He reasoned carefully, since he knew that a miscalculation, such as he had made for Gary, would end those events that had begun when Euclid's Dry Cleaning and Dyeing truck had passed under his window. Mathilda went from the hospital to a restaurant and then to a movie, and it was the cleaning woman who told her, when she got home, that he had passed away.

The World
of Apples

Asa Bascomb, the old laureate, wandered around his work house or study—he had never been able to settle on a name for a house where one wrote poetry—swatting hornets with a copy of *La Stampa* and wondering why he had never been given the Nobel Prize. He had received nearly every other sign of renown. In a trunk in the corner there were medals, citations, wreaths, sheaves, ribbons, and badges. The stove that heated his study had been given to him by the Oslo P.E.N. Club, his desk was a gift from the Kiev Writer's Union, and the study itself had been built by an international association of his admirers. The presidents of both Italy and the United States had wired their congratulations on the day he was presented with the key to the place. Why no Nobel Prize? Swat, swat. The study was a barny, raftered building with a large northern window that looked off to the Abruzzi. He would sooner have had a much smaller place with smaller windows but he had not been consulted. There seemed to be some clash between the altitude of the mountains and the disciplines of verse. At the time of which I'm writing he was eighty-two years old and lived in a villa below the hill town of Monte Carbone, south of Rome.

He had strong, thick white hair that hung in a lock over his forehead. Two or more cowlicks at the crown were usually disorderly and erect. He wet them down with soap for formal receptions, but they were never supine for more than an hour or two and were usually up in the air again by the time champagne was poured. It was very much a part of the impression he left. As one remembers a man for a long nose, a smile, birthmark, or scar, one remembered Bascomb for his unruly cowlicks. He was known vaguely as the Cézanne of poets. There was some linear preciseness to his work that might be thought to resemble Cézanne but the vision that underlies Cézanne's paintings was not his. This mistaken comparison might have arisen because the title of his most popular work was *The World of Apples*—poetry in which his admirers found the pungency, diversity, color, and nostalgia of the apples of the northern New England he had not seen for forty years.

Why had he—provincial and famous for his simplicity—chosen to leave Vermont for Italy? Had it been the choice of his beloved Amelia, dead these ten years? She had made many of their decisions. Was he, the son of a farmer, so naïve that he thought living abroad might bring some color to his stern beginnings? Or had it been simply a practical matter, an evasion of the publicity that would, in his own country, have been an annoyance? Admirers found him in Monte Carbone, they came almost daily, but they came in modest numbers. He was photographed once or twice a year for *Match* or *Epoca*—usually on his birthday—but he was in general able to lead a quieter life than would have been possible in the United States. Walking down Fifth Avenue on his last visit home he had been stopped by strangers and asked to autograph scraps of paper. On the streets of Rome no one knew or cared who he was and this was as he wanted it.

Monte Carbone was a Saracen town, built on the summit of a loaf-shaped butte of sullen granite. At the top of the town were three pure and voluminous springs whose water fell in pools or conduits down the sides of the mountain. His villa was below the town and he had in his garden many fountains, fed by the springs on the summit. The noise of falling water was loud and unmusical—a clapping or clattering sound. The water was stinging cold, even in midsummer, and he kept his gin, wine, and vermouth in a pool on the terrace. He worked in his study in the mornings, took a siesta after lunch, and then climbed the stairs to the village.

The tufa and pepperoni and the bitter colors of the lichen that takes root in the walls and roofs are no part of the consciousness of an American, even if he had lived for years, as Bascomb had, surrounded by this bitterness. The climb up the stairs winded him. He stopped again and again to catch his breath. Everyone spoke to him. *Salve, maestro, salve!* When he saw the bricked-up transept of the twelfth-century church he always mumbled the date to himself as if he were explaining the beauties of the place to some companion. The beauties of the place were various and gloomy. He would always be a stranger there, but his strangeness seemed to him to be some metaphor involving time as if, climbing the strange stairs past the strange walls, he climbed through hours, months, years, and decades. In the piazza he had a glass of wine and got his mail. On any day he received more mail than the entire population of the village. There were letters from admirers, propositions to lecture, read, or simply show his face, and he seemed to be on the invitation list of every honorary society in the Western world excepting, of course, that society formed by the past winners of the Nobel Prize. His mail was kept in a sack, and if it was too heavy for him to carry, Antonio, the *postina*'s son, would walk back with him to the villa. He worked over his mail until five or six. Two or three times a week some pilgrims would find their way to the villa and if he liked their looks he would give them a drink while he autographed their copy of *The World of Apples*. They almost never brought his other books, although he had published a dozen. Two or three evenings a week he played backgammon with Carbone, the local padrone. They both thought that the other cheated and neither of them would leave the board during a game, even if their bladders were killing them. He slept soundly.

Of the four poets with whom Bascomb was customarily grouped one had shot himself, one had drowned himself, one had hanged himself, and the fourth had died of delirium tremens. Bascomb had known them all, loved most of them, and had nursed two of them when they were ill, but the broad implication that he had, by choosing to write poetry, chosen to destroy himself was something he rebelled against vigorously. He knew the temptations of suicide as he knew the temptations of every other form of sinfulness and he carefully kept out of the villa all firearms, suitable lengths of rope, poisons, and sleeping pills. He had seen in Z—the closest of the four—some inalienable link between his prodigious imagination and his prodigious gifts for self-destruction, but Bascomb in his stubborn, countrified way was determined to break or ignore this link—to overthrow Marsyas and Orpheus. Poetry was a lasting glory and he was determined that the final act of a poet's life should not—as had been the case with Z—be played out in a dirty room with twenty-three empty gin bottles. Since he could not deny the connection between brilliance and tragedy he seemed determined to bludgeon it.

Bascomb believed, as Cocteau once said, that the writing of poetry was the exploitation of a substrata of memory that was imperfectly understood. His work seemed to be an act of recollection. He did not, as he worked, charge his memory with any practical tasks but it was definitely his memory that was called into play—his memory of sensation, landscapes, faces, and the immense vocabulary of his own language. He could spend a month or longer on a short poem but discipline and industry were not the words to describe his work. He did not seem to choose his words at all but to recall them from the billions of sounds that he had heard since he first understood speech. Depending on his memory, then, as he did, to give his life usefulness he sometimes wondered if his memory were not failing. Talking with friends and admirers he took great pains not to repeat himself. Waking at two or three in the morning to hear the unmusical clatter of his fountains he would grill himself for an hour on names and dates. Who was Lord Cardigan's adversary at Balaklava? It took a minute for the name of Lord Lucan to struggle up through the murk but it finally appeared. He conjugated the remote past of the verb *esse*, counted to fifty in Russian, recited poems by Donne, Eliot, Thomas, and Wordsworth, described the events of the Risorgimento beginning with the riots in Milan in 1812 up through the coronation of Vittorio Emanuele, listed the ages of prehistory, the number of kilometers in a mile, the planets of the solar system, and the speed of light. There was a definite retard in the responsiveness of his memory but he remained adequate, he thought. The only impairment was anxiety. He had seen time destroy so much that he wondered if an old man's memory could have more strength and longevity than an oak; but the pin oak he had planted on the terrace thirty years ago was dying and he could still remember in detail the cut and color of the dress his beloved Amelia had been wearing when they first met. He taxed his memory to find its way through cities. He imagined walking from the railroad station in Indianapolis to the memorial fountain, from the Hotel Europe in Leningrad to the Winter Palace, from the Eden-Roma up through Trastevere to San Pietro in Montori. Frail, doubting his faculties, it was the solitariness of this inquisition that made it a struggle.

His memory seemed to wake him one night or morning, asking him to produce the first name of Lord Byron. He could not. He decided to disassociate himself momentarily from his memory and surprise it in possession of Lord Byron's name but when he returned, warily, to this receptacle it was still empty. Sidney? Percy? James? He got out of bed—it was cold—put on some shoes and an overcoat and climbed up the stairs through the garden to his study. He seized a copy of *Manfred* but the author was listed simply as Lord Byron. The same was true of *Childe Harold*. He finally discovered, in the encyclopedia, that his lordship was named George. He granted himself a partial excuse for this lapse of memory and returned to his warm bed. Like most old men he had begun a furtive glossary of food that seemed to put lead in his pencil. Fresh trout. Black olives. Young lamb roasted with thyme. Wild mushrooms, bear, venison, and rabbit. On the other side of the ledger were all frozen foods, cultivated greens, overcooked pasta, and canned soups.

In the spring a Scandinavian admirer wrote, asking if he might have the honor of taking Bascomb for a day's trip among the hill towns. Bascomb, who had no car of his own at the time, was delighted to accept. The Scandinavian was a pleasant young man and they set off happily for Monte Felici. In the fourteenth and fifteenth centuries the springs that supplied the town with water had gone dry and the population had moved halfway down the mountain. All that remained of the abandoned town on the summit were two churches or cathedrals of uncommon splendor. Bascomb loved these. They stood in fields of flowering weeds, their wall paintings still brilliant, their façades decorated with griffins, swans, and lions with the faces and parts of men and women, skewered dragons, winged serpents, and other marvels of metamorphoses. These vast and fanciful houses of God reminded Bascomb of the boundlessness of the human imagination and he felt lighthearted and enthusiastic. From Monte Felici they went on to San Georgio, where there were some painted tombs and a little Roman theater. They stopped in a grove below the town to have a picnic. Bascomb went into the woods to relieve himself and stumbled on a couple who were making love. They had not bothered to undress and the only flesh visible was the stranger's hairy backside. *Tanti, scusi,* mumbled Bascomb and he retreated to another part of the forest but when he rejoined the Scandinavian he was uneasy. The struggling couple seemed to have dimmed his memories of the cathedrals. When he returned to his villa some nuns from a Roman convent were waiting for him to autograph their copies of *The World of Apples.* He did this and asked his housekeeper, Maria, to give them some wine. They paid him the usual compliments—he had created a universe that seemed to welcome man; he had divined the voice of moral beauty in a rain wind—but all that he could think of was the stranger's back. It seemed to have more zeal and meaning than his celebrated search for truth. It seemed to dominate all that he had seen that day—the castles, clouds, cathedrals, mountains, and fields of flowers. When the nuns left he looked up to the mountains to raise his spirits but the mountains looked then like the breasts of women. His mind had become unclean. He seemed to step aside from its recalcitrance and watch the course it took. In the distance he heard a train whistle and what would his wayward mind make of this? The excitements of travel, the *prix fixe* in the dining car, the sort of wine they served on trains? It all seemed innocent enough until he caught his mind sneaking away from the dining car to the venereal stalls of the Wagon-Lit and thence into gross obscenity. He thought he knew what he needed and he spoke to Maria after dinner. She was always happy to accommodate him, although he always insisted that she take a bath. This, with the dishes, involved some delays but when she left him he definitely felt better but he definitely was not cured.

In the night his dreams were obscene and he woke several times trying to shake off this venereal pall or torpor. Things were no better in the light of morning. Obscenity—gross obscenity—seemed to be the only fact in life that possessed color and cheer. After breakfast he climbed up to his study and sat at his desk. The welcoming universe, the rain wind that sounded through the world of apples had vanished. Filth was his destiny, his best self, and he began with relish a long ballad called The Fart That Saved Athens. He finished the ballad that morning and burned it in the stove that had been given to him by the Oslo P.E.N. The ballad was, or had been until he burned it, an exhaustive and revolting exercise in scatology, and going down the stairs to his terrace he felt genuinely remorseful. He spent the afternoon writing a disgusting confession called The Favorite of Tiberio. Two admirers—a young married couple—came at five to praise him. They had met on a train, each of them carrying a copy of his *Apples*. They had fallen in love along the lines of the pure and ardent love he described. Thinking of his day's work, Bascomb hung his head.

On the next day he wrote The Confessions of a Public School Headmaster. He burned the manuscript at noon. As he came sadly down the stairs onto his terrace he found there fourteen students from the University of Rome who, as soon as he appeared, began to chant "The Orchards of Heaven"— the opening sonnet in *The World of Apples*. He shivered. His eyes filled with tears. He asked Maria to bring them some wine while he autographed their copies. They then lined up to shake his impure hand and returned to a bus in the field that had brought them out from Rome. He glanced at the mountains that had no cheering power—looked up at the meaningless blue sky. Where was the strength of decency? Had it any reality at all? Was the gross bestiality that obsessed him a sovereign truth? The most harrowing aspect of obscenity, he was to discover before the end of the week, was its boorishness. While he tackled his indecent projects with ardor he finished them with boredom and shame. The pornographer's course seems inflexible and he found himself repeating that tedious body of work that is circulated by the immature and the obsessed. He wrote The Confessions of a Lady's Maid, The Baseball Player's Honeymoon, and A Night in the Park. At the end of ten days he was at the bottom of the pornographer's barrel; he was writing dirty limericks. He wrote sixty of these and burned them. The next morning he took a bus to Rome.

He checked in at the Minerva where he always stayed and telephoned a long list of friends, but he knew that to arrive unannounced in a large city is to be friendless, and no one was home. He wandered around the streets and, stepping into a public toilet, found himself face to face with a male whore, displaying his wares. He stared at the man with the naïveté or

the retard of someone very old. The man's face was idiotic—
doped, drugged, and ugly—and yet, standing in his unsavory
orisons, he seemed to old Bascomb angelic, armed with a flam-
ing sword that might conquer banality and smash the glass of
custom. He hurried away. It was getting dark and that hellish
eruption of traffic noise that rings off the walls of Rome at dusk
was rising to its climax. He wandered into an art gallery on the
Via Sistina where the painter or photographer—he was both—
seemed to be suffering from the same infection as Bascomb,
only in a more acute form. Back in the streets he wondered if
there was a universality to this venereal dusk that had settled
over his spirit. Had the world, as well as he, lost its way? He
passed a concert hall where a program of songs was advertised
and thinking that music might cleanse the thoughts of his heart
he bought a ticket and went in. The concert was poorly attended. When the accompanist appeared, only a third of the
seats were taken. Then the soprano came on, a splendid ash
blonde in a crimson dress, and while she sang *Die Liebhaber
der Brücken* old Bascomb began the disgusting and unfortunate
habit of imagining that he was disrobing her. Hooks and eyes,
he wondered? A zipper? While she sang *Die Feldspar* and went
on to *Le temps des lilas et le temps des roses ne reviendra plus* he
settled for a zipper and imagined unfastening her dress at the
back and lifting it gently off her shoulders. He got her slip
over her head while she sang *L'Amore Nascondere* and undid
the hooks and eyes of her brassiere during *Les Rêves de Pierrot*.
His reverie was suspended when she stepped into the wings to
gargle but as soon as she returned to the piano he got to work
on her garter belt and all that it contained. When she took her
bow at the intermission he applauded uproariously but not for
her knowledge of music or the gifts of her voice. Then shame,
limpid and pitiless as any passion, seemed to encompass him

and he left the concert hall for the Minerva but his seizure was not over. He sat at his desk in the hotel and wrote a sonnet to the legendary Pope Joan. Technically it was an improvement over the limericks he had been writing but there was no moral improvement. In the morning he took the bus back to Monte Carbone and received some grateful admirers on his terrace. The next day he climbed to his study, wrote a few limericks and then took some Petronius and Juvenal from the shelves to see what had been accomplished before him in this field of endeavor.

Here were candid and innocent accounts of sexual merriment. There was nowhere that sense of wickedness he experienced when he burned his work in the stove each afternoon. Was it simply that his world was that much older, its social responsibilities that much more grueling, and that lewdness was the only answer to an increase of anxiety? What was it that he had lost? It seemed then to be a sense of pride, an aureole of lightness and valor, a kind of crown. He seemed to hold the crown up to scrutiny and what did he find? Was it merely some ancient fear of Daddy's razor strap and Mummy's scowl, some childish subservience to the bullying world? He well knew his instincts to be rowdy, abundant, and indiscreet and had he allowed the world and all its tongues to impose upon him some structure of transparent values for the convenience of a conservative economy, an established church, and a bellicose army and navy? He seemed to hold the crown, hold it up into the light, it seemed made of light and what it seemed to mean was the genuine and tonic taste of exaltation and grief. The limericks he had just completed were innocent, factual, and merry. They were also obscene, but when had the facts of life become obscene and what were the realities of this virtue he so painfully stripped from himself each morning? They seemed to be

the realities of anxiety and love: Amelia standing in the diag-
onal beam of light, the stormy night his son was born, the day
his daughter married. One could disparage them as homely but
they were the best he knew of life—anxiety and love—and
worlds away from the limerick on his desk that began: "There
was a young consul named Caesar/Who had an enormous
fissure." He burned his limerick in the stove and went down the
stairs.

The next day was the worst. He simply wrote F - - k again
and again covering six or seven sheets of paper. He put this
into the stove at noon. At lunch Maria burned her finger, swore
lengthily, and then said: "I should visit the sacred angel of
Monte Giordano." "What is the sacred angel?" he asked. "The
angel can cleanse the thoughts of a man's heart," said Maria.
"He is in the old church at Monte Giordano. He is made of
olive wood from the Mount of Olives and was carved by one
of the saints himself. If you make a pilgrimage he will cleanse
your thoughts." All Bascomb knew of pilgrimages was that
you walked and for some reason carried a seashell. When Maria
went up to take a siesta he looked among Amelia's relics and
found a seashell. The angel would expect a present, he guessed,
and from the box in his study he chose the gold medal the
Soviet Government had given him on Lermontov's Jubilee. He
did not wake Maria or leave her a note. This seemed to be a
conspicuous piece of senility. He had never before been, as the
old often are, mischievously elusive, and he should have told
Maria where he was going but he didn't. He started down
through the vineyards to the main road at the bottom of the
valley.

As he approached the river a little Fiat drew off the main
road and parked among some trees. A man, his wife, and three
carefully dressed daughters got out of the car and Bascomb

stopped to watch them when he saw that the man carried a shotgun. What was he going to do? Commit murder? Suicide? Was Bascomb about to see some human sacrifice? He sat down, concealed by the deep grass, and watched. The mother and the three girls were very excited. The father seemed to be enjoying complete sovereignty. They spoke a dialect and Bascomb understood almost nothing they said. The man took the shotgun from its case and put a single shell in the chamber. Then he arranged his wife and three daughters in a line and put their hands over their ears. They were squealing. When this was all arranged he stood with his back to them, aimed his gun at the sky, and fired. The three children applauded and exclaimed over the loudness of the noise and the bravery of their dear father. The father returned the gun to its case, they all got back into the Fiat and drove, Bascomb supposed, back to their apartment in Rome.

Bascomb stretched out in the grass and fell asleep. He dreamed that he was back in his own country. What he saw was an old Ford truck with four flat tires, standing in a field of buttercups. A child wearing a paper crown and a bath towel for a mantle hurried around the corner of a white house. An old man took a bone from a paper bag and handed it to a stray dog. Autumn leaves smoldered in a bathtub with lion's feet. Thunder woke him, distant, shaped, he thought, like a gourd. He got down to the main road where he was joined by a dog. The dog was trembling and he wondered if it was sick, rabid, dangerous, and then he saw that the dog was afraid of thunder. Each peal put the beast into a paroxysm of trembling and Bascomb stroked his head. He had never known an animal to be afraid of nature. Then the wind picked up the branches of the trees and he lifted his old nose to smell the rain, minutes before it fell. It was the smell of damp country churches, the spare

rooms of old houses, earth closets, bathing suits put out to dry
—so keen an odor of joy that he sniffed noisily. He did not, in
spite of these transports, lose sight of his practical need for
shelter. Beside the road was a little hut for bus travelers and he
and the frightened dog stepped into this. The walls were covered with that sort of uncleanliness from which he hoped to
flee and he stepped out again. Up the road was a farmhouse—
one of those schizophrenic improvisations one sees so often in
Italy. It seemed to have been bombed, spatch-cocked, and put
together, not at random but as a deliberate assault on logic. On
one side there was a wooden lean-to where an old man sat.
Bascomb asked him for the kindness of his shelter and the old
man invited him in.

The old man seemed to be about Bascomb's age but he
seemed to Bascomb enviably untroubled. His smile was gentle
and his face was clear. He had obviously never been harried by
the wish to write a dirty limerick. He would never be forced
to make a pilgrimage with a seashell in his pocket. He held a
book in his lap—a stamp album—and the lean-to was filled
with potted plants. He did not ask his soul to clap hands and
sing, and yet he seemed to have reached an organic peace of
mind that Bascomb coveted. Should Bascomb have collected
stamps and potted plants? Anyhow, it was too late. Then the
rain came, thunder shook the earth, the dog whined and trem-
bled, and Bascomb caressed him. The storm passed in a few
minutes and Bascomb thanked his host and started up the road.

He had a nice stride for someone so old and he walked, like
all the rest of us, in some memory of prowess—love or football,
Amelia or a good dropkick—but after a mile or two he realized
that he would not reach Monte Giordano until long after dark
and when a car stopped and offered him a ride to the village he
accepted it, hoping that this would not put a crimp in his cure.

It was still light when he reached Monte Giordano. The village was about the same size as his own with the same tufa walls and bitter lichen. The old church stood in the center of the square but the door was locked. He asked for the priest and found him in a vineyard, burning prunings. He explained that he wanted to make an offering to the sainted angel and showed the priest his golden medal. The priest wanted to know if it was true gold and Bascomb then regretted his choice. Why hadn't he chosen the medal given him by the French Government or the medal from Oxford? The Russians had not hallmarked the gold and he had no way of proving its worth. Then the priest noticed that the citation was written in the Russian alphabet. Not only was it false gold; it was Communist gold and not a fitting present for the sacred angel. At that moment the clouds parted and a single ray of light came into the vineyard, lighting the medal. It was a sign. The priest drew a cross in the air and they started back to the church.

It was an old, small, poor country church. The angel was in a chapel on the left, which the priest lighted. The image, buried in jewelry, stood in an iron cage with a padlocked door. The priest opened this and Bascomb placed his Lermontov medal at the angel's feet. Then he got to his knees and said loudly: "God bless Walt Whitman. God bless Hart Crane. God bless Dylan Thomas. God bless William Faulkner, Scott Fitzgerald, and especially Ernest Hemingway." The priest locked up the sacred relic and they left the church together. There was a café on the square where he got some supper and rented a bed. This was a strange engine of brass with brass angels at the four corners, but they seemed to possess some brassy blessedness since he dreamed of peace and woke in the middle of the night finding in himself that radiance he had known when he was younger. Something seemed to shine in

his mind and limbs and lights and vitals and he fell asleep again
and slept until morning.

On the next day, walking down from Monte Giordano
to the main road, he heard the trumpeting of a waterfall. He
went into the woods to find this. It was a natural fall, a shelf of
rock and a curtain of green water, and it reminded him of a
fall at the edge of the farm in Vermont where he had been
raised. He had gone there one Sunday afternoon when he was
a boy and sat on a hill above the pool. While he was there he
saw an old man, with hair as thick and white as his was now,
come through the woods. He had watched the old man unlace
his shoes and undress himself with the haste of a lover. First he
had wet his hands and arms and shoulders and then he had
stepped into the torrent, bellowing with joy. He had then
dried himself with his underpants, dressed, and gone back into
the woods and it was not until he disappeared that Bascomb
had realized that the old man was his father.

Now he did what his father had done—unlaced his shoes,
tore at the buttons of his shirt and knowing that a mossy stone
or the force of the water could be the end of him he stepped
naked into the torrent, bellowing like his father. He could
stand the cold for only a minute but when he stepped away
from the water he seemed at last to be himself. He went on
down to the main road where he was picked up by some
mounted police, since Maria had sounded the alarm and the
whole province was looking for the maestro. His return to
Monte Carbone was triumphant and in the morning he began
a long poem on the inalienable dignity of light and air that,
while it would not get him the Nobel Prize, would grace the
last months of his life.

A Note on the Type

This book was set on the Linotype in Janson, a recutting
made directly from type cast from matrices long thought to
have been made by the Dutchman Anton Janson, who
was a practicing type founder in Leipzig during the years
1668–87. However, it has been conclusively demonstrated
that these types are actually the work of Nicholas Kis
(1650–1702), a Hungarian, who most probably learned his
trade from the master Dutch type founder Dick Voskens.
The type is an excellent example of the influential and
sturdy Dutch types that prevailed in England up to the
time William Caslon developed his own incomparable
designs from them.

*Composed, printed, and bound by The Book Press,
Brattleboro, Vt.*

*Typography and binding design by
Virginia Tan*